Other books by db wolfe/martin:
available at www.wolfeanddaga.com

TRYING NOT TO DIE IN THE TROPICS

SOUTH OF CANCER, NORTH OF CAPRICORN

DROP DEAD ON RUE DAUPHINE

*The wrongdoer cannot do wrong without
the hidden will of all.*

– Kahlil Gibran

INTRODUCTION

ARUBA- 85 million years ago

The island of Aruba formed as many others in the Lesser Antilles would as well. Forces steady and slow, but with the combined energy many times greater than of any harnessing of the atom by man, would convene along the convergent plate boundaries of the African and South American plates in the creation of Pangea.

Masses of igneous and plutonic rock would metamorphose from ancient sea floor mantle at the very edges of the colliding plates creating unique landforms. One portion would become over millions of years the "one happy island" of Aruba.

Sea levels would rise and fall many times and soon the skeletons of micro-organisms would add their weight and vibrant colors to the mother rocks of the Mesozoic Era.

With endless wave action, unfaltering trade winds, glorious sunshine, and a favorable location of 12 degrees North 70 West in what would become the Spanish Lake during the European exploration, this little island, the same size of Washington, D.C., prospered over the years.

It would pass in ownership after Spanish control in 1499 to the Netherlands in 1636. Even temporary occupation of the Dutch north province by the French during the Napoleonic Era couldn't change this faraway place. The Little General's only lasting effect was an 1811 decree requiring the use of Dutch surnames and so it is still in Aruba.

First a 19th century gold rush and then a booming economy based on oil refining fed by endless amounts of the new gold stored in the Maracaibo Basin made this Caribbean jewel a profitable part of what remained of the Dutch colonies.

No economic base remains for all time. By the 1980's, this island with 68 km of shoreline covered in pink sandy beaches now relied greatly on tourism. Its location well south of the hurricane belt is helpful as well. Specifically, visitors from its North American neighbors brought a modern type of gold, a paper gold with a shine of green.

However, there was another form of gold brought by the visitors. This gold is remindful to those of Dutch heritage of the motherland. To others who are likely of Spanish or Caribe Amerindian descent, it is exotic. This gold is long and flowing from the heads of young women.

This human gold attracts Aruban men like hummingbirds to nectar. They call the females who have it; 'yellowtails'. It is a common type of tuna in the Caribbean waters. A type of fish hunted daily and in great numbers. Yellowtail's hidden meaning is a derogatory term when directed towards, in local male eyes, the lesser gender.

The women that possess the flaxen tresses seem blithely unaware or genuinely impressed with the new attention. In many cases, that is all it is. But for significant numbers of young women visiting the third world, estranged from families and lovers or striking out on adventure for the first time in life, this gold marks them as targets. They are assets to those with dark hearts.

The rules governing the game played by men and women have changed and no one has told the visitors. This leaves them unarmed for the attacks that will come. These attacks will come, not with weapons, but with smiles, and more guileful methods, effective on young naïve hearts. It is pure Darwinism in micro-time and space.

I

HILTON HEAD ISLAND, SC   2006

All had been quiet since the Dolphin Affair as Wolfe liked to call it. Most Americans had no idea and never would about how close the United States came to being economically crippled. Most didn't even behave as if there were a war going on with two fronts and one of those turning sour fast. Somehow we managed to overthrow a dictator, occupy a country drowning with oil and not understand the history and culture well enough beforehand to not be caught in a civil war. We went in undermanned, unable to control the borders, and now were being victimized by Iranian supplied terrorists in training.

Wolfe scratched his head. The less he thought of it the better he could handle it.

"Hey, you!" Daga pushed his shoulder and the cold beer he was drinking missed Wolfe's mouth.

"Yes?" answered Wolfe innocently as he spit what beer had found his lips onto Daga.

"Hey! "Chu crazy?" Daga jumped to her feet in a mock fighting stance.

"Not at all." Wolfe replied calmly as he swept her feet with his and she fell into his arms.

Her warm, brown softness instantly melted to him and the sea breeze blowing steady from the SE caressed their bare skin. He tried to kiss her but she blocked his lips with a single, soft finger.

"What were you thinking when I pushed you?" Daga's blue eyes burned in to his like a perfect bolt of lightning. There would be no candy-coating this time.

"I was thinking about Iraq and since I can't do anything about it except vote out the liars, I started thinking of Aruba as well."

"You mentioned Aruba back in New Orleans. If it will keep you from thinking of the other thing, I'm all for it." Daga had long ago forbade Wolfe from thinking about Iraq because of the black cloud that soon encased his face and personality when he did. She didn't even use the word *Iraq.*

"Well you know this won't be a vacation. There's something that needs done and I'm tired of waiting for others. I'll tell you more about it as we go but we will still be able to enjoy ourselves a little. I'm ready when you are. Oh, by the way, we're sailing there. It's a little present I've owed you since we had to sell the *Peligroso.*"

"Oh! Wolfe!" cried Daga and the pair rolled in the sand of North Forest Beach. These were Wolfe's old stomping grounds since the 80's and where he returned like an echo down a canyon, a place always proven to be tried and true.

"Come on. Up and at 'em. We got to get your gear before we push off."

The boat floated gently in the tidal waters in Palmetto Bay. It sashayed like Stella in New Orleans with an easy movement, eye-catching but natural. Wolfe had named the boat *Lou-Lou* after Daga had related to him all that had happened with her bayou buddy.

The emerald green water framed the sleek hull and white sails as no artist could. She was a 40 foot ketch with a wooden hull and teak decks. Wolfe could hear Daga gasp.

"Wolfe! She's almost like *Peligroso*. She's beautiful!" Daga swung her arms around Wolfe's neck and her feet in the air. The pair nearly fell into Broad Creek.

"I hoped you would like it. She's all yours. I spent some of our ill-gotten poker money on her. Sam helped a little bit. Kinda. He never asked for any money to be returned!" A smirk walked easy across Wolfe's face. He loved it when everything came together just right.

"Is she seaworthy, and with stores? Daga yelled as she scrambled up the gangway and onboard temporarily forgetting about Wolfe.

"Absolutely. All taken care of. All you got to do is point and steer."

"We're sailing Wolfe. There'll be work mucho. Vamos?!"

"As soon as you stow all your gear. Mine's ready."

"You charted our route?" The question demonstrated La Capitana in Daga coming back on line.

"Mi querida. It's approximately 2200 miles as the crow flies but we're taking the Centro-American Caribbean coast and it'll be about 4500 miles at an average speed of 12 knots. I figure a little over two and half weeks, actual sailing time not counting any stopovers and adventures."

"Well come on. Vamos. Let's break it in?"

"It is in broken in! Some old sea dog used it as a live-aboard and a charter down in St. Thomas."

"I know it's broken in that way! I mean for us." Daga scrambled down the mid-ship hatch as her clothes landed on the deck. Wolfe smiled, shook his head, and gleefully followed as well.

The sailing was easy and the living was good. They stayed in the intra-coastal which protected them from any errant early spring storms and headed leisurely toward the The Keys before slipping out into the Straits of Florida. The day Daga and Wolfe spent navigating the Gulf Stream required Wolfe's best remembrance of vectors in physics class.

The warm water of the Gulf is forced to squeeze through at Cape Sable, Florida while headed up the East coast. This creates a fast-moving current much like when one places one's thumb over the hose mouth and the water picks up force and speed.

"Daga, keep a heading of 235 so we can cross the stream in the shortest distance." Yelled Wolfe above the noise of the wind and flapping sheets while struggling to trim the sails.

"Claro, my Wolfie. I've been here before." Daga responded.

They both knew that to sail West in the straits required crossing the Gulf Stream as directly as possible or no headway could be made. But in order to do so, one had to calculate the eastward flow of the current and time spent exposed. Basically, they were steering SW in order to go due South. Soon enough they and *Lou-Lou* were across and headed to the Yucatan channel while hugging the north Cuban coast.

Sunset performed its usual curtain call mesmerizing Wolfe and Daga. The colors were rich in the red spectrum and turned all things onboard a beautiful hue. Then suddenly, while sitting on the horizon, the sun melted out of sight and only a twilight glow reflecting off the clouds gave away its position.

Wolfe checked the GPS and quickly glanced to port. "Daga! Change heading to 270. We're a little off course and we wouldn't want to be paid a visit by Fidel's buddies. You know, suspected of being smugglers of people or dope."

"Yes, mi querida. Did you see something on radar?"

"No. No big deal. We get to about 85 W and we can turn and head towards Cozumel. We haven't had a real shower and meal since we left so why not."

"Sounds good. Get some rest. I'll need you at 2400h." Daga responded.

"Aye, aye capitana. See you in about four." Wolfe headed below decks and Daga turned her complete attention to the sea.

II

Many people think of pirates as both romantic and adventurous but the truth about them exposes what is a lowly life. If one were to ask about pirates, most would say they existed in the Caribbean and harassed the treasure fleets of the Spanish Main. True, yes, but only in part.

They were common criminals who happened to ply their trade on the sea. The dress they wore often included colorful handkerchiefs and golden earrings but anything more exotic would be worn by the captain and would have been captured from a ship and be part of the spoils.

One redeeming factor was the democratic election of the captain from the remaining crew if the previous captain had been lost in battle or otherwise disposed. However, pirates existed anywhere in the world where unarmed merchant ships heavily loaded with goods plodded along from seaport to seaport. The corsairs of the Mediterranean or the pirates of the South China Sea were nothing but opportunists stealing goods and selling crews into slavery.

Females, onboard captured ships, met the expected fate before being sold as concubines or kept by the captain. Crews resisting were hacked to death by cutlass or hanged from the mast. Walking the plank is nothing but an interesting literary tool.

Common methods for capturing ships were not what one might expect. Broadsides at point blank range were for the navies of Britain or Spain. Pirate ships were fast for both attack and getaway. They attacked only when the ship was low in the water or unarmed and were quick to exit when Corvettes or other likely opponents appeared on the horizon.

Trickery was not above these lowly types. Flags of the world's navies could be mustered from below when one was needed to entice a ship closer. Flying the colors upside down signaled distress until the unsuspecting Good Samaritan for a captain had sealed his and everyone's fate aboard.

The most common misconception about pirates if one were to ask a passerby on the street is they are history, an interesting but violent episode which interfered with commerce if one were European. If one were indigenous, it interfered only with who would be the one to benefit from native suffering.

Piracy and slavery are currently very much alive and well in all parts of the world. The Malaysian and Indonesian navies are in constant battles with pirates in the Maluca Strait. This passageway is the most heavily traveled merchant ship route on the seven seas.

For those who believe that slavery happened once and only then in West Africa, the Vatican recently issued a statement to the effect that involuntary servitude is at its highest level of activity than at any time in history. Although the integrity of the Vatican rests at an all time low, in these statements they are accurate.

These captives aren't made to work plantations but instead are used as boy soldiers and sexual assets. It was to these facts that Daga raised her binoculars to the horizon. She quickly went below decks to awaken Wolfe.

"What, baby? It's not 2400 yet is it?" He glanced at his watch. 2350h glowed back at him.

"There's a boat approaching fast. I can't tell if it's military or not. High speed."

"Where are we?" yelled Wolfe. He scrambled up on deck to see for himself.

"22N81W." Daga grabbed the binoculars again. The approaching boat had cut the distance between them by a third.

"That's not Cuba. Show me the boat." Wolfe swung the glasses to his eyes. It was a go-fast boat commonly used by smugglers and the running lights were off. If not for the phosphorescence of the wake and the minimal silhouette from available light, it would have gone unseen. Daga had saved the day.

"Open the aft deck locker! Bring everything! Wolfe tied the helm to a cleat in both directions. The *Lou-Lou* would stay on course without human hands.

Daga struggled back towards Wolfe, her arms heavily laden with necessary items. The approaching boat closed within 1000m.

"Here put this on." Kevlar body armor with a breast plate came flying back at Daga as Wolfe grabbed the weapons, chambered rounds, and looked forward at the boat that came out of the night.

He handed Daga the 12 gauge Mossberg 500 shotgun. "Take the safety off. Pull the trigger. Pump. Pull the trigger again. You have seven shells. Don't shoot unless I do. Understood?"

"Mierda! Que pasando!" Daga had reverted to her Spanish. A telltale sign for Wolfe could be no clearer.

"You shoot when I shoot! Got it! Quit thinking! Do what I tell you!"

"Shoot who!?" Daga had no confidence with firearms. She fondled her friend at the base of her neck.

"The pirates, best I can tell. We'll know in about 30 seconds."

Wolfe examined his weapons. He holstered the Baretta 9 mm and locked and loaded the M4 assault rifle. Short-barreled for in-close fighting, it weighed but 3kg with a 30 round mag of 5.56 ammunition. Capable of a fire rate of 700 per minute, few survived their first dance with it. He stacked twenty other magazines around the deck near his cover. He looked up to see the enemy.

The searchlight illuminated the *Lou-Lou*'s deck blinding anyone watching. Wolfe heard the throttled engine decrease in power and could make out the wake from the boat approaching them.

Daga hid below the gunwale unseen and Wolfe stayed motionless behind a folded sail and locker mid-deck. The bullhorn crackled alive.

First in Spanish and then in English, the commands came.

"This is the Cuban patrol boat *Mentiroso.* You are in Cuban waters. We will board you and escort you back to Cuba. Show yourselves and prepare to be boarded."

Wolfe double-tapped the glare that handcuffed his eyesight and then, opened up on full automatic across the boat's deck. A line tossed intended for securing the *Lou-Lou* shredded in mid-air. Daga stood and started blasting with the 12 gauge.

The helmsman hit the throttle to escape the surprise attack. The return fire was minimal. Wolfe continued to fire at the water line hoping to disable the engine and weaken its chances for survival.

"Daga! You OK? Daga!" Wolfe ran to the gunwale where Daga had been.

She sat slumped against the side breathing from the adrenalin rush and smiling.

" What? Chu think they scare me? I like this weapon. I know I blasted one of them. Adios, amigo for sure."

"Why didn't you answer me?"

"I'm trying to get my breath. You OK, mi querido?"

"Yeh, I'm OK. I hope it's only local thugs. Probably come out here a few times a week and pirate unsuspecting rich Americans. Sell the boats, ransom the people, keep the luxury items depending on whom or what is on board."

"How'd you know they weren't for real?"

"Legitimate navies give plenty of notice so as not to create an accidental firefight and don't use that type of boat. Pirates rely on surprise. They arrive in the middle of the night, crew asleep or heavily fatigued. It's a bluff that works most of the time. We won this round but we don't know if they have buddies. I've got the helm. Try to get some rest. We'll head 225 South and try to get to Cozumel in 12 hours or so. Sleep tight."

"How did you know to bring the weapons?"

"At the very least, this is drug running country. People go missing every year. It's always easier to be armed unnecessarily than to be unarmed in need. You know we're not *in Kansas anymore.*"

"What?" Daga asked.

"Nothing. Never mind. Go to bed. See you later."

"OK. But don't use up all your energy being a captain. I need you for a cabin boy, too." Daga winked and made a show of squeezing her exquisiteness down the hatch to Wolfe's pleasure and pain simultaneously.

III

COZUMEL

Daga motored the *Lou-Lou* up to the dock in Cozumel uneventfully. The giant cruise ships moored in the distance still cast long shadows in the late morning light. The walkways and sidewalks teemed with tourists eager to leave a little bit of America here in exchange for silver jewelry and Cuban cigars. Cozumel couldn't claim to be authentic Mexican anymore than Hawaii could claim to be American. The Norteamericanos had invaded with McDonald's and Hooters and while enjoying the spoils hadn't seen the Mexicans adding their special touch. It reminded Wolfe more of Key West after the Marielitos than of descendents of fierce Aztec warriors.

Daga and Wolfe started the walk toward town and as he expected, all work on the pier came to a screeching halt. Wolfe smiled to himself. They weren't ready for this Dominican priestess.

Her blouse clasped its long, sea-island cotton threads to every curve of her torso outlining for all the men who stared just how good God's handiwork could be. The java wrap sarong captured her hips in an embrace about which the longing faces at work could only fantasize. It wouldn't be long now.

"Oye! Chica! Como va? 'Chu want me? No?" This relatively polite verbal assault by the bravest of onlookers made the remainder fearless. The high-pitch whistles began accompanied by the sucking of teeth. Daga waited until she came near a group of dock men who until her arrival had been loading one of the cruise ships.

"Listen to me those who understand. You wouldn't last but a minute with me. You're chicos pretending to be hombres. 'Chu afraid to do but eager to yell. Todos están maracóns!" Daga glared back.

She had called them all faggots. Their machismo had been derided, this could not stand. It definitely could not from a woman. A swarthy, tall one stepped from the back of the crowd. Others began to encircle Wolfe in order to isolate him.

The self-appointed spokesman had been in a few fights at the waterfront. A scar ran diagonally under his left ear and stopped at the corner of his mouth accenting the curl of his lip. He took one more step at Daga before he spoke.

"Tu estás una puta americano. Un hija de puta. Una perra!" He didn't have time to smile.

The knife she kept taped to her spine always gave Daga great comfort. The blade flashed through the sunlight and nestled at the foolish one's neck before he realized it. Daga braved his foul breath and body odor and leaned in closer. His sweat now pouring into his eyes, he blinked uncontrollably. Daga shook her head at the group to move away from Wolfe. Slowly the half-circle receded.

"Chicos, today I am nice. Not always. Your compadre will live. But maybe castraste, huh?" The sharp edge began to move slowly down the man's torso. It stopped at his diaphragm. She leaned in once more. "Hoy vivas, mañana quizás."

By this time Wolfe had made his way back toward Daga. She released the foolish one, chuckling at the others as she did.

"Come on Wolfe. Little boys. I need a drink." The pair turned and walked toward town headed to Carlos and Charlie's.

The men shrank back in their shame and the shadows while shaking their heads, wondering where that woman with the devil blue eyes and African skin had been born. They knew without knowing it couldn't be America.

The entrance to Carlos and Charlie's faces the waterfront and is divided into restaurant or bar ingress. The clock hands barely showed afternoon. The noise level approached ear-damaging and the behavior of the patrons resembled a roadhouse in Carolina at closing time.

As usual, all male eyes and some female ones followed Daga and Wolfe to the bar. The thoughts behind those eyes one could only speculate, but it boiled down to what to do with Daga and how to get rid of Wolfe. Alcohol is the weapon of choice.

"Two beers, please. Coronas. Bottles. Do not open them." Wolfe ordered with a smile. He wanted to watch the predators.

Wolfe leaned over to the object of interest. "Daga, everybody speaks English. Mexican Spanish if you wish. You see how I ordered those beers?"

"Yes. And?"

"That is the only way to order drinks here. Don't take anything from an open container, from a friendly new acquaintance, a floor person, nothing. Understood?"

"Drugs in the drinks, I guess?" Daga shrugged.

"No guess. Drugs in some of the drinks. No way to tell which ones. Therefore the precautions. Not usually during the daytime because most of the customers are off cruise ships. Nighttime is a different matter. After that *baile* on the dock, no chances."

"Wolfie, I really need something stronger than beer. Rum, you know?" The rolled 'r' in rum seemed to have its own lifetime. Daga guzzled the last of the beer. Wolfe shook his head.

"OK. Tranquilo. Easy. I'll buy a whole bottle. What we don't drink, we'll give away. I'll order and I'll pay. Cool?"

"Cool." Somehow when Daga said *cool* it sounded so much *cooler.*

Wolfe ordered from the bartender a bottle of Cruzan rum unopened. Two glasses, no ice, and a whole lime accompanied the sugar cane liquor. Daga's knife would do.

"Here you go. Enjoy." Just as the bottle arrived, so did an uninvited guest.

She was cute. Her heritage showed her to be a Mixto in mexicano idioma. She had part Spanish, part Mezclo Indian in her veins. Genetically, a real hybrid would describe her.

The four grandparents of her bloodline constituted eighty percent of the Mexican gene pool.

"You want?" She yelled, while gesturing with an open bottle of some shooter made of tequila. It was the unknown ingredients that bothered Wolfe.

She gyrated in her t-shirt shaking her breasts in Wolfe's face but spending a little more time doing the same with Daga. Wolfe whispered in his querida's ear.

"Take the shot. Don't swallow. After she gives you the shooter, she'll slap your ass and grab your boobs from behind. Pretend to enjoy" Daga nodded in confirmation.

Daga did as Wolfe instructed. The floor server danced away with some money and a smile.

"She'll be back or one of her buddies. Here! Spit the drink on the floor." Wolfe moved his legs out of the way.

"You think anything could be in there?" Daga asked.

"Maybe HGB. Meanwhile, watch how they work the room. The young, naïve girls without males get most of the attention and most of the shots. Classic MO. Females that work on cruise ships don't go anywhere without males with them. They know."

"What the hell is HGB?"

"It's the latest date rape drug. HGB is more difficult to detect than roofies by victims since the manufacturers of Rohypnol put a color indicator in roofies so it changes to bright blue in contact with ethyl alcohol."

"What about HGB? Does it change color?" asked Daga.

"Nope. Gamma Hydroxy Butarate is tasteless, odorless, and colorless. Looks like water. Even a beginning chemistry student knows not to assume that liquids that look like water may not be. Vacation partiers aren't in that mind set. Works fast as well."

Wolfe shook his head as he thought of Aruba.

"Faster than rum?" asked Daga as she slugged another dark shot of Cruzan.

"Oh yeh. 10-15 minutes the effects begin. They last 3-6 hours without alcohol and 36-72 hours with alcohol. All traces leave the body within 72 hours and blood is not tested for presence of GHB in routine toxicology scans. It's even manufactured by the body and in some individuals in amounts equal to those when ingested."

"Don't the girls know what happened? If someone did that to me, his mother whore would cry over his spilled blood." She took another drink.

"Some of them kind of remember. Like a real bad alcoholic blackout. Some think it's a dream. Some think they remember but are ashamed or are on their way back home before becoming convinced they were raped. Hell, if it weren't for stupid criminals, nobody would get caught."

"What do the anos stupidos do, Wolfe?" The rum bottle was more than half gone and Daga was slipping into more Spanish.

"Well, there's the famous case of Andrew Luster. This guy is an heir to the Max Factor fortune...."

"The whaaaat?" Daga began to slur her words.

"Slow down on that rum for awhile, how about it? Anyway, this guy is at least a multi-millionaire living in SoCal at the beach. Picks up girls nearly everyday. Brings them back to his seaside pad. Good looking guy, wealthy, like shooting fish in a barrel.

But some of the girls have disturbingly long periods of blackouts. Some evidence of having had sex like soreness or body fluid deposits. But nobody remembers. Anyway, he's convicted of using GHB for rape because he videotaped his sessions with the women and kept the tapes. A lot of this information came out in trial. He skipped bail but Dog the bounty hunter caught up with him in Mexico." Wolfe waved the shooter girl away with a hand and a stare. She didn't seem happy. Daga didn't notice.

Daga's eyes were barely open. She lifted her head to look in Wolfe's eyes. "You'd protect me, querido?" She asked as she slumped into his lap.

"I'll protect you, baby doll." He whispered. Wolfe paid the tab. He half-dragged and carried Daga back to the boat. The dockworkers sneered in agreement that maybe gringos pick up women the same way as they do as well.

After tucking Daga comfortably in the rack and locking up the boat, Wolfe headed to the farmacía to test his theory. It didn't take long. Displayed in plain view and advertised in Spanish and English were a few dozen drugs. Wolfe knew most labels to be controlled substances in the USA.

On shelves not far from one another were drugs for erectile dysfunction, anabolic steroids, and GHB in anhydrous-salt form. All do have legitimate clinical uses but in most of the third world one is able to self-prescribe therefore bypassing the doctor.

The drug companies know that the drugs end up on the street because written prescriptions in the USA don't match usage amounts and manufactured output. This demonstrates perfectly the nexus between survival of the fittest and un-tethered capitalism.

Wolfe chuckled to himself. He'd be OK. The ones about whom he worried were the young ones that hadn't run the gauntlet of youthful ignorance and survived, the youths who possessed adult money but without adult experience.

He checked the prices. All were well below US prices and certainly within the economic reach of a criminally inclined male with plentiful potential victims at hand. Back to the boat he headed, for a good nap and an outgoing tide.

Daga woke with a cotton mouth but an urge to cook. Wolfe rubbed his belly in anticipation. Out on deck she prepared the feast. There'd be a big, fat meal before going out to sea once again. The food would be Caribbean while possible and she made a few runs to the waterfront for ingredients while noticeably un-accosted by lookers-on.

What she created would be worthy of a royal court. Out on deck Wolfe relaxed with rum and late afternoon sun as Daga cranked up her cooking skills. Before he could finish his drink, Daga presented Wolfe with a platter of coconut shrimp.

Heavily breaded with sweet, flaky coconut meat and then dipped in lime-mustard sauce, the shrimp quickly transported Wolfe back to the days when he had first met Daga in St. John, USVI.

The next course came with tuna salad and slices of seared raw Ahi in mixed greens, sweet peppers, and lemon-vinaigrette dressing. Finally, Daga delivered the coup de grace, Pescado Havana sautéed in latin-chorizo sauce with capers and garlic-herb butter.

Both inhaled the food, literally, using first the sense of smell and sight, and succumbing lastly to the palate and instinctual hunger.

Unlike Americans, food is as much a sensual pleasure as sex to those of Mediterranean persuasion. Daga wouldn't allow Wolfe to be anything but the one who shared her bliss. Afterwards, Wolfe would return the favor with only enough time allowed between food and fun for his belly to return to a normal shape.

IV

OFF THE EAST COAST, CENTROAMERICA

The weather played its part and the seas as well. Sailing could be so relaxing and then in moments threaten one's life. So far all had gone well. Wolfe navigated *Lou-Lou* far enough from shore not to be easily noticed but close enough to be somewhat in sheltered waters.

Soon they passed Belize and its capital, stopping instead at the Islas de la Bahia SE of the Gulf of Honduras for re-supply and relaxation. These islands are more like outposts than cities or towns. They did their best to not draw much attention, answering few questions from homesick Americans or anyone else. Rested and replenished, they headed for the Nicaraguan coast and Costa Rica beyond.

Far enough south to be out of danger of even the earliest of hurricanes, Wolfe and Daga anchored in the Golfo de los Mosquitos for some fun and fresh fish as well. Despite its less than inviting name, the Mosquito Coast off northern Panama is a nature lover's delight.

"What 'chu doin', baby?" The exaggerated *chu* signaled to Wolfe on what Daga intended to spend time this day. She planned to enjoy a few of her favorite pleasures.

"I'm fishing. You want fresh fish for dinner, don't you?" Wolfe tossed the net over the stern. The coral reefs crawled with delicious specimens. However, the best specimen wouldn't be ignored.

"Wolfie! Aquí! Por favor!" The words were unnecessary.

Daga stood up at the bow where she'd been sunbathing. Nude, with a glass of rum in her hand, she could have been one of so many mermaids on the bowsprits of boats. None ever carved by man looked like this heavenly form.

Her skin, darkened by the days at sea and dripping sweat in rivulets down muscle-carved canyons and switchbacks only a higher being could have made, beckoned Wolfe uncontrollably. The fish would be safe for awhile.

Lying in one another's arms on deck in a lover's rapture, Wolfe heard an engine approaching. Dressing quickly he grabbed the shotgun.

"Daga, put something on! Some one is coming. Hurry! Grab that coconut!"

"But Wolfie, we were just about to play some more."

"Now! Daga! Get the coconut."

She managed to do as she was told but in her mind she pondered all the things Wolfe would have to do to make up for this interruption.

"OK. I've got the coconut. Now what?"

"Throw it up in the air as high as possible. Away from the boat. Ready? Go!"

The nut thrown by Daga would never put out someone at home plate but it accomplished its task. Wolfe hit it with a shotgun blast as if it were part of an ancient form of skeet. The pieces floated down and scattered across the water. The engine of the approaching boat throttled back and then turned away. Wolfe leaned on the rail.

"What was that all about? I hope it was important?" Daga already began to remove her suit again.

"I didn't want visitors of any kind. Friendly or pretending to be so. Pirates come in all shapes and sizes. I figured the coconut demonstration would be enough to change his mind. Coconuts, you know, resemble the shape and size of human skulls. I think he got the message."

"Well since you're so good at sending messages, I hope you can read this one." Daga got down on the deck and crawled the few feet between them exaggerating her movement as if she were a female jaguar. From his response, Wolfe read the message well.

"Where we going now?" Daga asked as she hoisted the anchor line.

"Take a heading of 14 degrees NE. Should take us where we want to be." Wolfe watched as Daga swung the *Lou-Lou* around and took a direct route to Aruba.

ORANJESTAD, ARUBA

Daga settled the *Lou-Lou* in her berth not far from the cruise ships in Aruba's capital. The city of Oranjestad reminded one of gingerbread cookies and brightly colored dirndls of Bavaria although Aruba is a Dutch protectorate. This is not to say that modern influences had not had an effect over the island. Neon light beer signs and drug-addled individuals roaming the streets held almost equal sway to the quaint architecture.

Once Wolfe squared away the boat and the pair cleaned up, it seemed the perfect time for a preliminary tour of the terrain.

Wolfe hailed a taxi, negotiated a rate, one which he new had its origins in the driver's imagination and relative need for cash, and proceeded to give Daga a geography lesson.

"Alright, Daga. We're on the mid NW coast. The island is approximately 28 miles long and about 8 miles wide at the extremes. 68 square miles, about 50% larger than Hilton Head. It points NW and is shaped like a paramecium."

"A what?"

"Doesn't matter. Like a bedroom slipper."

Daga nodded her head as if she understood but Wolfe new his explanation was lost in translation and might have been even if English were her first language.

Wolfe gave directions to the driver. "Head up Smith Boulevard North, past the hotel stretch, out to California Point. Then come on back past Oranjestad and head in the direction of the airport."

"Why you wan' go there?" The driver seemed suddenly tense. Wolfe noticed the hunched shoulders, Daga did not. She instead contented herself by staring out the dusty windows at the desert-like landscape highlighted in the distance by hotel facades and coconut palms.

"Where? California Point?" Wolfe decided to do some intel.

"Yeh, mon. All sorts of Americans been down there two years now, all over this island really. Looking for that girl. You here for that?" the driver's head seemed on a swivel as he tried to drive and see Wolfe's face simultaneously. Wolfe, of course, obliged his efforts by scooting into the middle of the back seat so as to make the man's attempts hopeless.

Wolfe gave the standard non-answer answer. "Do I look like someone who cares about another missing woman in the Caribbean? That's like caring about sand in the desert. I'm here to gamble and party and if you have any suggestions I'll listen."

"Just, you know mon, there's been a lot of....."

"I don't care. Just follow my directions, please."

The remainder of the ride turned quiet except one conversation the driver had on his cell. Spoken in papiamento, the local Creole, Wolfe didn't understand the contents, only that it had been very animated and the word *Americanos* had been spoken frequently.

Finally, they arrived at Wolfe's choice of restaurant.

"Come on Daga. Tonight and tonight only. We're going to splurge. A little something French and after tonight we stick to Aruban or American cuisine if the word cuisine can be associated with American junk food prepared over seas." Wolfe chuckled to himself. Americans travel the world and then struggle to find the McDonald's so as to have a taste of home.

Wolfe paid in cash, got the driver's card for the return trip to the marina, and the pair walked to the door of Chez Mathilde. Located between Oranjestad and the Reina Beatrix Airport at the Sonesta Hotel complex at Havenstraat, the restaurant offered true French cuisine. Seated immediately, Wolfe could order his favorite dish, in French, of course.

"Daga, permit me to order for you as well?"

"Of course, but everything has a price!" Her smile ran across her face, slowly at first and then all at once. Wolfe allowed himself to be captured.

Le serveur, no one called the help garcon anymore, arrived tableside.

"Monsieur, pour le deux. Bouillabaisse et une bouteille de pinot noir. Je prefer de California. C'est tout."

"Mais, monsieur…"

"Monsieur, c'est tout. Tu comprends?"

"Certainment." The transplanted frenchy lifted his chin while turning on his heels better than a Nazi SS sturmtruppen.

"What was that all about, Wolfie?"

"Nothing, Daga. One-upmanship. I won the first round. He may win the second. I ordered us seafood stew and a bottle of California pinot. Here at Chez Mathilde, the bouillabaisse contains twelve different creatures of the deep."

"You know what seafood does to me, Wolfe?" Daga's hand began to crawl up the inside seam of Wolfe's trousers.

"I'm very aware. That is, of course, why I ordered for you as well."

The two lovers managed to finish their meal and wine without causing the gallic gawkers at surrounding tables not to be "shocked, simply shocked." as Captain Renault might have been. Daga fell asleep on the ride back to the boat.

PLAYA LINDA

Wolfe left Daga sleeping contently in her berth and headed to one of the casino hotels on the NW shore. He soon encountered for who he had been looking.

"You sure you want to double down against a face?"

The handsome, blonde man signaled the dealer again that he indeed desired another card. "Just deal, please. No questions."

The dealer exposed and delivered to the man's total of 10 another face.

"See! Why not? I've got a good hand."

"Becau—se," the dealer drew out his words slowly as he exposed both his cards,

"I have blackjack." He collected the cards while showing little or no emotion. Not the case for the player.

The game being played was not identical to the one so well known in America. It was European blackjack sometimes known as *no peek.* The dealer does not expose his hand if he indeed has blackjack because the dealer has not looked or even dealt himself a second card. From the management point of view, it is difficult to have a tell about a hand one knows nothing about. Yes, even blackjack dealers have tells. Some intentional, most are not.

In this manner, if players are foolish enough to double against a face or ace, they lose both bets. In the American game, one knows the dealer does not have blackjack before any third cards are dealt. Doubling against a face or an ace remains a questionable play, but one does not risk double one's original wager to find out the dealer has the perfect hand.

"Call over Klaas. I need another marker. Five thousand USD."

The dealer waved over the pit boss as he had been instructed. A large, square man who at one time of his life could have been classified by scientists as a pure mesomorphic specimen in the realm of Mike Tyson approached. An oversized head squared at the top by a blonde crewcut and piercing blue eyes complemented the intended message first announced by his physique. The muscles in his face flexed as if he were controlling his emotions and in so doing allowed Wolfe to see a distinguishing mark. The faded scar ran from behind his left ear and disappeared below his straining shirt collar at the carotid artery. Two knife cuts to the face on two different people in a week or so. Welcome to the third world.

Scarring from the *cuchillo,* the blade, has an easy explanation in the rest of the world away from the USA. Unless one is in law enforcement or a member of a criminal organization, handguns are hard to come by and carry severe penalties for possession especially by non-citizens. Killing is somewhat rare for it requires some determination on the part of the person wielding the knife to finish the job. Guns make killing easier. Persons in a rage, who may only have wounded a victim with a knife, become murderers instead.

The politeness in the boss's voice sounded rehearsed rather than genuine. The difference would have been lost on the player.

"Klaas. I need five K."

"That will put you at 25K this week. Would you care to discuss this in private?"

"No, I would not. Before I leave tonight we will talk. OK?"

"As you wish." Klaas signaled the dealer to cash the marker he provided.

The dealer in turn provided the usual good service. "All black or some purple?"

"All purple. My luck is not too good tonight. I need to double up."

"Certainly." The plum-colored chips worth five hundred USD each were soon stacked neatly in front of the player and not in the betting circle. A total of ten disks glared back at the player. Both Klass and the dealer mentally shook their collective heads in wonderment. If one were to say they had poker faces, it would be an under statement.

A common error in gambling and especially in blackjack or sports is *to go for it*, double and triple up because eventually one is bound to win. This is not necessarily so.

This faulty logic assumes too many variables that may or may not be true in the player's favor, the most glaring of which, is she or he has an unlimited bankroll. The majority of players do not.

"Well, at least bring in new cards. I paid for them!"

It had been expected. Klaas nodded at the dealer who was already reaching for the shoe.

As the dealer shuffled and re-shuffled the cards, Wolfe sat down at the table.

"Mind if I play?" Wolfe asked.

"Why not? Maybe my luck will change." Wolfe wondered if even in Aruba this guy was old enough.

"Well, while he's shuffling. I'm Wolfe." He introduced himself while extending his hand.

"My name is Dirk." The introduction and handshake both were perfunctory.

"You live here?"

"Yes. My entire life. I'm losing at this moment. I believe he is ready to deal."

"So he is." What an ass thought Wolfe. So young, as well. How bad could it be? He soon found out.

In less than thirty minutes, the twenty-something, had lost the five K. As is usual in his age group, he slammed the table, belittled the employees, and couldn't figure out how he had lost. The Dutch kid stormed from the pit. Wolfe shared a half-smile with the dealer.

"Does he play often?" As he asked, Wolfe noticed the pit boss intercepting Dirk at the exit and escorting him to an unmarked door.

"Play? Yes. Win? No." The two enjoyed a laugh.

"He looks kind of young?"

"He's old enough now. His father is a lawyer big time on the island. Works for the government. They allowed the son to play when he was under age."

"Why would they do that?"

"Why not? If there are any problems with the authorities, we're even. It's like money in the bank."

"How much does he lose? He just lost five K in front of me."

The dealer rolled his eyes, verbally silent.

"I understand." Wolfe nodded. "The old man pays?" Wolfe checked to see if the pit boss had returned. The door remained closed.

The dealer eschewed an oral response once again. However, the face didn't lie.

"All of it?" As he asked the question, Wolfe slid a black chip toward the dealer.

Gladly accepted and properly deposited in the tip box attached to the side of the table, the dealer reached to his left which allowed him to glance around undetected for the boss.

"Some of it. Then he cut him off. I don't know how he does it now."

As Wolfe and the dealer finished their conversation, Wolfe noticed the pit boss and Dirk exiting the private office. The discussion seemed heated and Wolfe could make out Dirk exaggerating the words *no problem.* The tall, handsome youngster threw open the glass portal and hurried away. The boss returned to the pit. Wolfe started first.

"Everything OK? I'm Wolfe." Wolfe leaned forward to affect a handshake. A catcher's mitt-like paw enveloped a portion of the American's wrist while shaking his hand.

"Welcome to the Casino Bonito. I'm Klaas Bruin at your service. Why do you ask?"

"Your facial features. You seem upset."

"Not at all. Thinking about a girl."

"We all suffer, don't we?" A communal tribal grunt issued forth from the trio of XYers.

"Yes, indeed. How's he treating you?" Klaus nodded in the direction of the dealer.

"So-so. Ready to call it a night. Hey Klaas, you look like you know your way around a Smith Machine. Where's the best gym?" It was an honest question on Wolfe's part although with an ulterior motive.

"Downtown by the cruise ship terminal. Where are you staying?"

"Oh, same area." No need to be specific, thought Wolfe. "Thanks." Wolfe got up from the table and left. As he did so, the dealer and Klaas conferred.

Dirk happened to be Dirk Kuiper. He came into the world the son of a judge and despite his young age, he might be labeled a wealthy playboy although the term playboy implied willful participants. Sexual predator more accurately described his true behavior and possibly even worse, a murderer and rapist.

Wolfe knew the man's features well and so had joined him at the table. His face had been seen all over the world. He was one of the reasons Wolfe and Daga were in Aruba.

V

EAGLE BEACH

The sound of the slapping water keeping its rhythmic beat combined with sweet tropical air is the best alarm clock in the world. It had the same effect on Daga. She stretched her muscled yet sleek torso till she nearly bumped Wolfe from the berth onto the deck of the boat. "Come on, baby. What we doin' today?"

"To the beach. Nothing more. All we got to do is party and act like we're here to have a good time. Make some friends and keep our ears open." Wolfe hipped her back to her side. The first points scored were by Daga. Hulk Hogan might call it a submission pin.

The drive up the west coast of the island went quickly and shortly the pair sauntered out on the white sand as 1100h approached. Wolfe picked a spot up from the wooden pier. One could purchase sundries and tourist junk there, as well as, there were a few open-air restaurants and bars.

As soon as Wolfe began to drag some chairs to their spot, the beach attendant appeared and picked up the rent. He hung around for a few minutes explaining where everything could be found. His patience didn't go un-rewarded as Daga decided to accommodate the young man's hopes. She began to uncover. Wolfe sat down and watched from behind his dark glasses.

She and Wolfe had decided they needed to be noticed straight away. Daga played the part that would be the eye candy that attracted the drones. She wore a halter leopard print swim top stretched to a place its designer hadn't imagined. A Brazilian-cut white thong covered the other regions although covered seemed a misrepresentation even if one were from Rio.

When the boy-man recovered his breath before needing medical attention, he scurried away to inform the rest of the pack of his newfound treasure. Daga and Wolfe exchanged knowing glances.

"Well, you'll be on the list of new bait tonight at all the bars."

"I'm old enough to be his mother!" Then realizing the import of what she said Daga followed with a belated qualifier. "Not quite!"

"Don't worry, grandma." Wolfe teased. "You're plenty young for them but you do have a problem."

"What, my bootie? I'm just, how your American musicians say, bootalicious?" Even Daga succumbed to the endless insecurity of females and their form. Never to be discouraged by males or the media in so doing.

"Not your body, Daga. You've got a man. I wouldn't be surprised if somewhere along the way they try to separate the bull from the cow."

"Such a romantic metaphor. You loco sometime, baby."

"You know what I mean." Wolfe knew he stepped in it.

"Si, si, I know. And you—you will know... lonely!"

A day of sun later as the temperature slouched toward 80, Daga and Wolfe headed to the bar at the pier. It didn't take long.

The bartender practically choked on the piece of pineapple in his mouth when Daga and Wolfe saddled up to the bar. Rushing over to the pair, he threw a bev nap in front of Wolfe and settled in front of Daga, gingerly placing the napkin on the bar, and mentally removing what little covering she had with his eyes. Wolfe could have been a talking bottle palm tree. The bartender saw only Daga.

"Some nice cool rum drinks for my American friends?"

"Sure." answered Wolfe forcefully, finally drawing the attention of the bartender. "You don't get pretty women around here?"

"All the time."

"This is Daga. She is mine. We'll take two piña coladas. No umbrellas, no rude fellas, and everyone calls me Wolfe."

"El Lobo, huh?" the bartender answered as he moved away to make the drinks.

"Not El, just Wolfe. What's your name?"

"Denys."

Wolfe chuckled. Denys. A perfect name for a bartender. It's a derivative of Dionysius, Greek god of the grape harvest.

"What's so funny, mon? You no like my name?" Denys's ego, like those of many men and especially those in the Caribbean, had been bruised if ever so slightly. If it had not been bruised, slightly brushed would do the trick.

"No man, we're cool. It's that you have a perfect name for a bartender. It comes from the god of the harvest.

"I see." Denys's body language relaxed and he finished making the drinks. "Where you get such a beautiful woman?" he spoke to Wolfe as if Daga had disappeared or wore a FOR SALE sign on her ample chest.

Wolfe didn't have time to respond. Daga beat him to it. "Remember, no rude fellas. Where's a good place to go this evening for some partying?"

Denys, at first steamed by Daga's remark, took a moment to reconsider, and responded in a soft voice.

"Go downtown. Plenty of places there."

Wolfe and Daga finished the drinks and headed back to the taxi stand.

"Great guy, right? He's probably already making a call." The words spit from Wolfe's mouth indicated his disgust.

Daga nodded in agreement. Game on.

VI

GUANTANAMO BAY, CUBA

Sam Sauria made the starboard turn at Windward Point and headed in to the sweet confines of Gitmo Bay. No one called it Guantanamo. This pronunciation required too many syllables. A perfect breeze filled the sail and the sloop headed gently toward the marina on the windward side. Once he tied her up with a short walk to the Tiki Bar and Sam's day will have been as good as it gets.

The evening interrogation sessions would begin soon enough. A few drinks to wash away the disturbing feeling he experienced whenever he had to work inside Camp Echo wouldn't hurt anything. Although, his visits and drinks were becoming more and more frequent lately.

Camp Echo held the *ghosts.* The enemy combatants that the International Red Cross didn't know about by name or knew by false names given to them by the Joint Detention Operations Group. J-DOGs seemed to be the perfect acronym for the soldiers that worked there. These were guards who looked forward to reporting for duty.

The questioners were of another ilk. All of the interrogators were graduates of Huachuca, the Army's school for training inquisitors. The Defense Language Institute came later for vocabulary and cultural immersion. All these soldiers were 97 Echo. Highly trained, motivated, and given a blank slate to gather intelligence anyway possible.

The prisoners required extremely high security and according to the JIG, Joint Intelligence Group, held high level intelligence information crucial for the USA's success in the war on terror. Three terrorist attacks and ultra level information leading to the capture of some of the notorious *deck of 52* had been garnered from Camp Echo. Inside that wire someone knew where Osama and al-Zawahiri took their meals. Abu Ghraib, comparatively speaking, seemed like a holiday resort.

Sam was a bit of an outsider; OGA. It served as the GITMO acronym for *other government agency* so the letters CIA wouldn't be uttered or the overused nickname of The Company as well.

Sam had booked a session with a familiar face but the gloves were about to come off. He, of course, wouldn't be the perpetrator of illegal tactics. Sauria had learned the lesson of plausible deniability well. He'd get the intel, if possible, and if any heat came down the pike the army would take the hit. After Abu Ghraib, the public and the Pentagon could be duped without much imagination. They wanted to believe it must have been sociopathic soldiers from small towns in West Virginia rather than the top brass or the President himself who ordered the torture.

Sam's co-interrogator had been part of Task Force 121 in Iraq, the Special Ops teams that ran down Sadaam and

Zarqawi. There'd been too many curious JAG lawyers after awhile when prisoners starting dying and men believing in the Geneva Conventions began asking about missing teeth, burns, and bruising on prisoners. So Sam's helper got shipped to GITMO where the spotlight wasn't dim. It didn't exist at all.

Sam passed all the security measures and signed in for his prisoner using a non-descript name each time. Today he wrote down Bill Green. He waited patiently for the J-DOGs to bring the hapless soul to the interrogation room.

The J-DOG opened the interrogation room and ushered Sam to the table. The PUC today had at one time been the chief of Al-Qaeda in SE Asia. Pronounced *puke* by the guards, PUC represented *person under control* and illustrated how far Rumsfeld and the Pentagon would go to never acknowledge the detainees in a manner that might be argued qualified them for protection under the rules of war as taught in the service academies.

Up until now Sam had been the good cop managing to prevent others from harming the detainee. Today he would ask the questions, wait for answers, and watch.

The warm feeling from the alcohol in his stomach comforted him in this distasteful task.

He wanted the intel but he knew extracting it in this manner had negative side effects. He rationalized it by remembering that PUC's just like today's subject had killed themselves and others gruesomely without thought about rules made by infidels.

The door opposite Sam swung open and the prisoner entered. Chained with shackles and manacles with a connecting chain through his legs, he walked with the familiar prison shuffle. All-clasping links fastened finally to a heavy leather belt resembling a weightlifter's, his posture gave away the fact he hadn't been broken psychologically. Today would be the day, thought Sam.

The dark hood he wore had only a single opening for a mouth making the prisoner look like a half-finished

Mr. Potato Head or worse a Hollywood version of a condemned man. Today it might be true. The J-Dog removed the captive's hood revealing just how far Camp Echo reached in an attempt for information.

Bruises circled his face giving it the countenance of a recently pummeled boxer. His beard had been shaved and he wore no prayer cap. All of the propaganda about allowing prisoners to practice their religion did not apply to the *ghosts*. Those media releases were for the blathering press. Denying religious practices is just another tool used to psychologically traumatize prisoners.

He spoke English well with the sing-song accent of an Indonesian. The J-DOG pushed him harshly into a wooden chair with no padding on the seat and spindles missing from the spine.

Sam spoke first, addressing him as only a number. "Good day, 14. Let us get started immediately. We are short on time and I have treated you well in the past. Today I do not have that luxury." Sam's eyes lingered on the bruises about the detainee's face for added emphasis.

The once powerful man snickered, holding on to his last vestiges of power and respect. It would do him no good. Sam continued.

"We know you were planning attacks before you became our guest." Sam let the irony of the statement hang in the air momentarily. "We know you were planning to use the *mubtakkar.*" The word translated to invention in English.

Try as he might to suppress all expression, the word mubtakkar had garnered an involuntary response from the prisoner. He would try now to lessen the damage with words.

"I know nothing of an invention. Sounds like infidel fantasies to me."

"I told you we didn't have time today." Sam stood and leaned against the wall.

At that signal, the door flew open and more guards poured into the room. Firstly, the soldiers replaced the hood.

Others cut the shapeless body shroud from the prisoner. There were only disparate pieces of remaining cloth dangling from his restraints.

His nude body showed more areas of physical abuse in the manner of his face. Another soldier placed a bucket of saline ice water at the detainee's feet. Two burley J-DOGS picked the prisoner up and placed him standing in the bucket. Sam stared back at him although the once chief of Al-Qaeda in SE Asia could not see. Sam tried again.

"Tell us about mubtakkar, 14."

"I have said I know nothing. How could I know something now because you infidels like to look at naked men and place me in ice water. This is why you will lose."

Everyone has something that is more than they can take. It is the job of the interrogator to find the key.

The German shepherd dog rushed in the door and while the guards held the prisoner upright, attacked. He bit first at the back of the knee, large chunks of tissue coming off in his mouth. Next, he gnawed at the portion of the lower leg exposed above the rim of the bucket. The screaming could be compared to rock concert decibel levels. The handler commanded the dog to heel.

"Once again, 14. Tell us about mubtakkar." Sam asked in an even voice.

The shoulders of the detainee slumped and he began to shake as the hypothermia and traumatic shock ravaged his nervous system. His entire physical demeanor became that of a dog beaten too many times by a newspaper and now required only the rattling of the weapon to induce compliance. He, hoping the Americans wouldn't allow the animal there, covered his genitals with both hands. He began to talk.

"It is simple."

"How so?"

"All that one needs one can get at WalMart and a college chemistry lab or as a janitor in a high school. The materials from the lab are so common one would never miss them."

Sauria motioned at the guards. They removed the hood, picked the detainee from the bucket and placed him on the chair. A medical tech placed bandages on the wounds and wrapped a warm compress around his feet. The prisoner's nearly frostbitten appendages were misshapen and gnarled like those of an arthritis sufferer. The color was completely gone. The tech hurried from the room while shaking his head as he wondered how one who had studied medicine in order to help people ended up in a place remindful of the Black Hole of Calcutta.

"Go on." Sam's features exhibited the perfect poker face. They gave away no information and definitely no emotion.

"It's a cyanide gas bomb in a duel system arrangement. Relatively stable in glass containers and when separated. A poisonous gas when the vials are ruptured and the reactants combine."

"The ingredients?" Sauria had to make this a homerun.

"Common household rat poison for the cyanide and hydrochloric acid for the other reactant. Makes hydrogen cyanide gas and is the size of a backpack. Runs off a dry cell battery for dispersion and that particular gas in a closed area like a subway car would have a 70% kill ratio."

"When and where?" asked Sam.

"Large cities. As soon as we get the packs past the rent-a-cops at the entrance. Our operatives are independent in that once they have constructed the bomb they may act when it is possible. Of course, we have an agreed upon time but that is only if all conditions are ideal as in the embassy bombings in Africa."

"That is where. When?"

"The next New Year's Eve."

Sam tried not to show the information had any effect. But Jesus, on the trains on the way to Times Square on Dec. 31!? Holy shit!

"And the antidote?"

"This you already know. Amyl nitrate or, of course, a physical barrier like a gas mask."

The session ended. The guards dragged the detainee with his useless feet out of the interrogation room. Sam barfed in the corner. He would rather kill them in a battle than torture them.

"What's a matter Mr. Green? No stomach for this stuff?' asked the remaining guard.

"Yeh, the rules of war keep getting in the way. Besides, when they get our guys what do you suppose they'll do?"

"What they've been doing. Burn them alive, string the bodies from a bridge, or behead them live on the internet. This is a whole new ballgame."

"You got a point. However, they win when we become them. In Texas, they like to say 'some people need shot'. This isn't shooting. This must have been what it was like during the Inquisition."

"Hell, Mr. Green, they're killing reporters and contractors by sawing their heads off. They've used large bit drills to bore into the base of the skulls of fellow Iraqis. Both Shi'a and Sunni alike. They're not human and I have no problem treating them as such."

"Che Guevara knew that terrorism worked best when one could cause through one's actions the enticement of the government to attack its own people, take away rights, ignore the constitution, and in so doing bring to the side of the rebels the very population the government meant to protect.

I think it's about page 34 in his famous treatise *Guerrilla Warfare* which worked quite well for terrorists in South and Central America throughout the 50's and 60's."

"Whose side you on, Mr. Green?" the J-Dog asked in total confusion.

"Ours, unfortunately." The answer increased the level of befuddlement in the enlisted man. He pulled out a notepad and scribbled a few words. He had standing orders to report such ramblings.

Sauria left the room and couldn't get back to his bungalow in Woodward Loop housing quick enough. To his neighbors, he masqueraded as a private contractor doing electrical work in the base residential areas. A worker that drank his share of Knob Creek bourbon.

While throwing back what would be his final drink of the evening, Sam shook his head in disenchantment. Both Khalid Shaikh Mohammed and Ramzi Yousef were trained in electrical and chemical engineering in the USA. They had taken perfect advantage of our open educational system. How had that happened?

These two masterminds were the brains behind both WTC bombings and the Bojinka plot out of Manila. The latter manifested as a plot to blow multiple planes out of the sky simultaneously en route to the USA from SE Asia.

A later plot, originating in Britain and scheduled for 2006 to blow up multiple planes en route to NYC, still used the engineering knowledge of Yousef although Ramzi now resided in the Supermax Prison in Colorado with fellow bombers Kazinsky and Rudolph. Sam, tasked to see just how far the technical information had spread throughout Al Qaeda, found himself unhappily at Guantanamo.

VII

ORANJESTAD

Wolfe had forgotten. Carnival season continued due to a late arriving Easter. Tonight would be one of the last "jump-ups". He and Daga would dress accordingly.

"Come on, baby. Let's find a catbird's seat before the parade begins."

Daga wore only white leather although at which point her skin stopped and the hide of the deceased mammal began were indistinguishable due to the small amount of leather used and the tightness of the outfit. It was a halter top with low-slung pants exposing her tight abdomen and exaggerating her fruitful hips. She mesmerized the crowd of not easily stunned carnival goers.

Her exposed nature trail, a line of semi-precious stones leading from her navel downward, interwoven with sun-bleached abdominal hair, caught the attention of security personnel. It gave the policemen ample opportunity to make sure Daga didn't possess any weapons.

The search of Daga consisted more about exploring her shape than smuggling illegal protection but she allowed it. She did, however, pack her usual companion in its customary location.

Wolfe as always provided deep contrast to his stunning companion with his taste in attire. He might as well have been a doorman at one of Jimmy Buffet's innocuous restaurants and bars. He wore a Del Sol mango-colored guayabera, the threads and icons changing color uniquely as the photosensitive chemicals embedded in the cloth reacted to the UV radiation.

Once past the useless security, Daga and Wolfe climbed to the top of the Burger King where outdoor seating on the rooftop provided an even better view of the street below.

"You know, Wolfe. It's a long time since I've been to a Carnival."

"Yes, querida. This will be fun for a while and then we will go track some predators. On a night like this, they should be out in full strength. We'll watch the "jump-up" first and if we're lucky we'll see the King and Queen of Carnival. Then we'll tend to business. Right now, let's have a few Mojitos."

"Real mojitos? The way mi abuelo made them?"

"Well, I don't know how your grandfather made them but I can guess that here in Aruba a few miles off of the coast of Colombia and Venezuela one might be able to get a mojito with cane juice and not powdered sugar!"

"Even aged Cruzan rum?"

"Yes, good dark rum as well." Wolfe placed the order with the waitress. His kind of Caribbean, Wolfe thought. One of the few places where one can order rum drinks at the Burger King.

While waiting for their drinks, faint wisps of the Bouyon music, the jump-up rhythm from Dominica, began to settle on his and Daga's ears. First the drums and then the bass, the sound could not be mistaken for some other. It had the effect of beginning to move you physically and one could look around and see tiny tots and teetering grandmothers beginning to swing their hips in pace with the beat.

The street filled with revelers, not organized costumed crewes. Soon every body, human or otherwise, would be moving to the music. No one could sit still and so it would be "jump-up" time.

The drinks came. The amount provided just enough to put them in the mood but not so much to interfere with the evening's business.

"Daga! Here comes the King and Queen of Carnival!"

"She's so beautiful! I could have been a Carnival Queen!" Daga made an exaggerated pout with her lips.

"Baby, that queen got nothing on you!" Wolfe and Daga embraced and kissed then wheeled around once more to admire the Carnival Royalty as they approached.

As in nature, the male had most of the plumage.

Dressed as M'Ganza, the Witch Doctor, King of Carnival guaranteed the lucky male plenty of female attention for the remainder of his life. Plumes danced from his headdress, down his moist arms nearly to his wrists, giving the impression of soon to be flight. The colors were the teal green and dark indigo of the peacock. Another set of feathers cascaded down his outer thighs and enveloped his ankles, giving the impression of a man-bird. The large beak of a fish hawk served as the focal point to the codpiece completing the costume.

The Queen showed demonstrably how less or nothing could be more. The palpable heat of the day rose from the street. Combined with the animal musk wafting from the writhing mass of humanity, the scene was surreal and sensual as well.

She rode high on the shoulders of bearers, the transporters all being capable of at least a mini-camp tryout for the NFL. She had light skin probably some mixture of Amer-Indian, Spanish, and African. She wore only the flag of Aruba in miniature over her areola though her nipples refused to be restrained by such light cloth. The Queen had become the crowd as it had become her.

Her headdress reflected the ambient light like spilled diamonds on a mirrored surface. Nearly three feet tall and made of emeralds embedded into South Asian silk, the crown seemed to wrap itself around her hair in the shape of a Bantu symbol of fertility.

The remainder of the costume consisted of a matching bejeweled thong whose front covered only enough territory to be discreet. To describe the view from the rear as she passed by, one would be required to spend more time and words in description than the designer did in its creation. She wore it well.

Her light brown skin glistened as the sweat beaded and then rolled down her unending limbs. For all intents and purposes, she ruled the island of Aruba that day.

The passing of the royalty caused the crowd to follow along and grow in size. By the time they reached the center of Oranjestad, nearly the entire population would be there.

"OK, Daga. What do you say? One more mojito and then off to work?"

"Si, Wolfie. But chu know that t'e mojitos and t'e "jump-up" have had t'eir effect on me!"

Heat, the tropics, jungle music, sensual costumes, and alcohol conspired to overtake Daga. Her telltale change of accent always indicated the transformation. Wolfe, of course, would be the beneficiary of Daga's unleashed passion. He smiled as he envisioned what his queen of the carnival would be like tonight. No other man could be as lucky as he. He'd take his queen over all others. They were perfect together as long as he accepted those things he knew were in her heart and soul.

Carlos' n Charlie's this night down on the waterfront could not contain its own crowd. The people spilled out on to the street. The revelers displayed in situ the Aruban version of what one associated with Roman bacchanalias.

People in various stages of inebriation stumbled around and into one another. Wolfe and Daga struggled inside to the bar. The doorman, in charge of checking ID's and for weapons, cared considerably more about the party than performing his task.

The joint heaved with Americans of both genders less than 18 years of age; lambs being led to the slaughter and happily so. Mostly inexperienced with alcohol or hypnotic compounds, these children of the well to do would learn much about the darker side of life before the sun's rays brought them back from the edge. A few might fall into the abyss never to return.

"Daga, remember. Drink only from the bottles of beer we order. The caps should be in place. Don't take any shots from strangers, workers or otherwise. Just watch without staring. If you feel you must point out something important, say it in French. That's probably the one language with which we can conceal the subject of our conversation."

"Voulez-vous coucher avec moi." Daga giggled as she spouted out the one phrase practically everyone understood in French.

"Daga!" Wolfe laughed as he wagged his finger at her. "You'll get yours. Just not now." Her demeanor, rather than a negative, allowed the pair to hide in plain sight. They were just a couple of inebriated Americans during Carnival. Wolfe filled the role of a typical white bread guy from Ohio who struggled to control his woman in the tropical steam.

As Daga took another swig of beer, Wolfe, while glancing through the triangular picture frame made from her bent elbow and the bottle, saw them enter.

He, of course, led the pack. Dirk Kuiper sauntered in to the bar on one of the wildest nights of the year and in less than a minute his party had a table. Wolfe noted the time, 2400h. It is a typical MO for predators.

The alcohol coursing through the circulatory systems of the intended victims would be beginning to pickle the cerebrum in all but the most experienced drinkers. First the fine motor skills of speech and writing are affected then the large motor skills of walking and balance. Finally, as the alcohol level approaches amounts that cause unconsciousness, memory loss occurs. Kuiper and his crew couldn't wait that long.

They wanted to hedge their bets much as Mark Furman did in the OJ case. They wanted to make sure.

One of Dirk's sidekicks motioned a server to the table. Money exchanged hands and the floor man hurried away. Kuiper's two companions looked as if they were brothers. Dark skinned and slight in stature and build, their bloodlines would run through Suriname back to Hindu descendants of East India.

The server returned with two open bottles of shooters; contents unknown.

Kuiper motioned at a table of blonde females well into a night of drinking. The body language could be read by any observer. The floor man explained that Dirk had bought the girls drinks. The Aruban nodded in acknowledgement as the server indicated that fact to the ladies.

Daga finished another beer. Wolfe struggled with watching the predators and keeping an eye on Daga as well.

He hooked his foot around her leg so if she moved from her seat or even looked over her shoulder he would feel it.

Wolfe could imagine the conversation at both tables. The men laughed about what they would do to the unsuspecting targets and the girls admired the handsome looks of Dirk. The girls believed they were only flirting. If flirtation described the situation, then the dalliance was with death.

Over the period of an hour, the usual tracking of the prey one sees on the African savannahs recreated itself in human terms. The server brought the table and chairs of the girls over to Dirk and his boys. The human hyenas displayed exaggerated smiles. The Arubans separated each girl from the others by placing themselves between them. The culling of the weak had begun.

Kuiper picked the prettiest of the three. From where Wolfe sat, she could have been an Ohio State cheerleader. Long, flowing, blonde tresses curled softly around her neck and fell effortlessly into her considerable cleavage. Her skin, brown from hours in the sun, contrasted perfectly with the light eyes and hair.

Alcohol flowed freely especially from the shooter bottles left conveniently by the server after another exchange of money. Then the hyenas made their move.

The entire group left the tables and headed outdoors. As they reached the pavement it looked as if it had been choreographed. Dirk went straight with his captive, although she hadn't guessed her status yet. The two brothers pulled their girls at three and nine o'clock respectively. In a about a minute, they had vanished in the crowd. Wolfe shook his head. Although he considered them lower than a snake's belly, their technique of corralling girls had been practiced and repeated many times successfully if this latest waltz was an indicator.

The women now separated from one another, likely in a drug and alcohol-induced blackout, would have no recollection of what would occur in the next few hours.

Wolfe focused on Daga. She needed to get back to the boat. He had seen what he had suspected. Now he needed a plan to execute.

"Come on, Daga. Time to go."

"What 'chu mean mi Wolfie? We're havin' one good time."

Not really, thought Wolfe. Their conversation had consisted of ordering more beers for the last two hours. "Come on, baby. I'm looking for my queen of carnival."

"Oo-la-la. Si, mi querido. It ees time for 'chu to be mi hombre."

Wolfe managed to get Daga below decks without injuring her. He tucked her in tightly so she couldn't roll out of the bunk. She made a final attempt to pull him to her and then collapsed backwards into her liquid dreams. Crawling on to the portside bunk, he lie awake fitfully till well past 0330h imagining what the girls were suffering. Alcohol and fatigue finally granted him some rest.

However, Dirk and his cohorts weren't in the mood for resting. They rendezvoused at the California Lighthouse in separate vehicles. Each of the three girls lay in weirdly similar positions in the backseats. Legs splayed apart, heads dangling at strange angles above the car floor, rag doll-like aptly described the condition of their repose. Their muscles completely without tonus and incapable of function, they could be positioned as wished. Soon the masters of these hapless marionettes would begin the performance.

They didn't think of themselves as criminals, but of course they were. The shooter bottles contained GHB. In the United States, possession of *liquid x* sufficed as prima facie evidence of intent to rape and its classification as a Schedule II drug carried minimum penalties of up to twenty years and a million dollars for possession of any amount regardless of quantity.

They had purchased the Gamma-OH legally at the pharmacy in Oranjestad just as Wolfe had seen it displayed in Mexico. Its legitimate medical purposes encompassed treatment for sleep disorders and alcoholism. In the third world, the pharmacist doesn't ask. The customer requests a specific drug and if it's not controlled, which very few drugs are, he purchases it.

The young men didn't become criminals under Aruban law until the rapes began. They took turns, repeatedly, but only after Kuiper had had the first go. Their early morning depravity was a modern version of cavemen dragging their intended mates by the hair. The difference was that Neanderthals, motivated somewhat by survival of the clan, had higher intentions than these modern miscreants.

The girls would come out of the blackouts in a couple of hours. They would awake nude, no clothing to be found. Hiding in the stand of sea grapes nearby, they would wait for female passersby and yell for help. Towels and cover-ups would be loaned gratefully and as the young Americans left in a taxi back to the hotel, the good Samaritans would shake their heads and giggle about that being the worst walk of shame they'd ever seen.

The girls would swear each other to total secrecy and in this instance mean it. As the days passed and they returned to the States, brief images of their torture would pop up in their consciences. Each one being more afraid than the other to even confide what they suspected.

In this manner, Dirk and his buddies plowed through the naïve bodies of young American girls. Kuiper, ringleader and alpha male especially in his mind, had as well another criminal agenda, one of which the others were unaware.

Each time the threesome performed their wicked samba of sex, Kuiper left the scene after the brothers. Volunteering to take care of things, he slipped instead into the darkest part of his soul in order to save his wretched self. Not every time, he rationalized, just once before and maybe one more in the future. They were stupid little girls with rich careless parents. Who cared? He didn't, of that he was sure.

VIII

THE MARINA

"Up and at 'em, baby!" Wolfe didn't expect an instant response from the pile of bones which constituted Daga.

A few shakes later, and she managed to move. "You find me weak and you take advantage. Not fair."

"I haven't taken advantage yet!" Wolfe rolled on top of her and they laughed. It is the good hearty laugh that brings you life. Times like these brought Daga and Wolfe to the intersection of their lives.

What would qualify as afternoon delight had the time been past noon instead became a naked brunch for lovers.

"OK. A little sun. Then I'm headed down to the casino across from the cruise ship terminal."

"I see how you are. Use me and lose me." Daga laughed. She knew he couldn't resist her.

"Gotta go. Last night while you were doing laps in a pool of Sol beer, I worked."

"Always working. I know."

"You catch on quickly. I'll be at the casino downtown once I give my back some sun."

They laid on the foredeck, Wolfe with his feet stretched toward the bowsprit and Daga in her royal elegance, nude behind the mainsail cover. If she hadn't used the area between the sail covers for discreetness, all commerce at the marina would have come to an abrupt halt.

Frozen mango drinks with Cruzan rum put Wolfe right where he wanted to be; mellow and napping in the sun. When Wolfe awoke from his siesta, he rolled over, gave Daga a peck on the cheek, and prepared for an afternoon of games of chance. Other, more deadly games might be played as well.

He dressed in Jimmy Buffet runway attire or at least Gilligan moderne. The shirt he wore had hemp plants in khaki on an olive background. His manila-colored linen pants with pleats completed the ensemble. He added a *Tres Hermanos* maduro cigar hand rolled from Nicaraguan tobacco. The *puro* became the perfect final detail of his facade. Wolfe entered Casino Royale and soon found what constituted the purpose of his visit.

Dirk sat at the blackjack table losing as usual. A fact Wolfe could ascertain before he arrived at the table. Easily seen from across the casino floor, the same antics and body language seeped from Kuiper as had when Wolfe first met him. Seeped described the behavior because it all came from a noxious, virulent source and carried the same characteristics as other types of excrement. The pounding fist and verbally abusing the dealer, all are part of the usual poor gambler's outward behavior. Dirk just was a particularly bad case.

Casinos don't allow extremely poor behavior unless they are making tons of money from the person. This Aruban apparently qualified under those conditions.

Wolfe saddled up to the table. "Mind if I play?" No response from the malefactor was forthcoming. Wolfe continued. "500$, please. Red and green." The dealer complied.

As the dealer counted the money and then the chips, Wolfe tried again with Kuiper. "Hey, didn't we play the other night together at the casino at Playa Linda?"

"Perhaps, briefly. Nice to see you again." A bit of thaw came off the tone of voice.

Wolfe's over-politeness began to have the intended effects. "It's Wolfe. You're Dirk, right?" Wolfe extended his hand.

"Yes. That's correct. You have a good memory." Kuiper managed to be cordial with the handshake as well.

"Well, if I remember correctly you're some kind of player. You didn't have much luck the other night but you sure know what you're doing. You know what they say, unlucky in cards, lucky with the ladies." Not quite, of course, but adapting a quote for his own purposes frequently happened with Wolfe when trying to schmooze a loser.

"Yeh, maybe that's what it is. I've been running very cold lately."

"Not with the yellowtails. I saw you with a hottie down town last night. She and some friends. How'd you do?"

"Yellowtails? I see you're familiar with our local endearment. You American?" Kuiper seemed much more interested in this portion of the conversation with Wolfe.

"All over. Military brat. Spent a lot of time in St. Thomas and St. Maarten. That's what we called them. Yellowtails. Anyways, how'd you do?"

"They were sufficiently entertained and sent home to their mommas."

A lascivious leer flashed for a moment and then a wider smile. Kuiper leaned over and high-fived Wolfe. The open hand acknowledgement had become another cultural export of America compliments of our entertainment industry. By the time high-fives were imitated in the third world no one even did them in America any longer. The soccer stadiums in Iran were just now beginning to do "the wave".

While this conversation had been occurring, Dirk had continued to lose and Wolfe had won. Numbers came easily to Wolfe and basic strategy blackjack isn't much different then counting. The American could play blackjack and carry on a complete conversation with multiple speakers and have very few misplays.

Wolfe's usual target of conversation at the blackjack table was the dealer. Hoping to create uncaught errors in his favor or spot tells in the dealer's voice, it could turn the odds positive to the player. Today the dummy was Dirk Kuiper instead.

"You're going to have to show me your technique with the women sometime." suggested Wolfe.

"I'll see you around. Buy you a drink maybe."

The two shook hands again and as Wolfe exited the floor he could again hear the ranting of a loser. Wolfe chuckled to himself. He wouldn't be accepting any drinks from the Aruban either.

Wolfe arrived back at the *Lou-Lou* to a crowd of spectators pointing and laughing.

He hurried aboard as the mostly male crowd began to disperse. He quickly saw what had created the commotion. Dear Daga had fallen into a deep slumber and rolled out from her protective nook in all her worldly wonder. How long the show had been going on, Wolfe had no idea. Even he took a moment before waking her. She was that spectacular.

"Come on baby doll. Wake up. You're lying nude out on the deck."

Daga sat up and gathered her senses. When what Wolfe had said sunk in, she turned and gave the last few stragglers still staring at her, a perfect double finger accompanied by a fury of curses in Spanish that even Desi Arnaz couldn't understand if he were alive.

She slipped her suit on while trying to kick Wolfe as well. "That's for laughing. I saw that smile. I know they're pendejos but you're just as bad."

"Oh, mi querida. I'm worse and you know it." With that silly remark, Wolfe disarmed Daga's anger and the two disappeared down the hatch. The *Lou-Lou*, shortly afterwards, began to make way although still firmly tied to the dock.

GITMO

A hand knocked loudly on the screen door of Sam's cottage, the racket jolting him from an afternoon dreamy vision. Two MP's packing sidearms stood at parade rest outside his door. Sam gathered himself and led the young grunts into his smallish kitchen.

"Gentlemen. I assume this isn't a date. State your business, gunney."

"Sir, you are to report immediately to Admiral Huck's office. Joint Task Force-Gitmo HQ, sir."

"Thank you for the message. Dismissed." Sam turned to gather his briefcase.

The young marines didn't budge. Sam positioned himself directly in front of the two faces. "Did you forget something, gunney? Need to use the head?"

"No sir. We are to escort you directly to the Admiral. Direct orders, sir." The movement of eyes and facial expression were absent, only the facts.

Admiral Howie Huck wanted to see Sam and it required two armed MP's. "I assume I'm not under arrest? It wasn't mentioned."

"No sir. Escort only. Our orders are to inform you of the Admiral's orders and to leave immediately without delay with you in our company."

"Will do." The three man party exited Sam's cottage without locking the door. A few miles ride down Sherman Avenue to the old McCalla Field went uneventfully.

Sam presented himself to the CPO clerk outside Huck's office. The marines stood a respectful distance to the rear. His presence was announced via office intercom and the CPO opened the intervening door to allow Sauria to enter. The grunts moved to either side of the entrance, executed an about face, and framed the door in America's finest.

The admiral stood and greeted his old classmate. "How the hell are you, Sauria. I hope there's been fair wind and a following sea."

"What's with the boys?" Sam jerked his thumb in the direction of the guards.

"A little extra security. Can't be too safe nowadays. Got a call from a friend of yours and it's an order. Understood?" The hint of a smile never birthed from its origins. The admiral's visage didn't budge.

Sam stood silently and stunned. He and Howie "Hooters" Huck had graduated from the academy together. "Hooters" Huck had gotten the moniker by wearing over-sized glasses and then removing the spectacles to peer more closely at well-endowed females. He looked like an owl and he liked large female breasts. The nickname was a foregone conclusion.

Sam searched his brain for anything he might have done. The illegal interrogations were like permanent markers in his mind's eye. "Who's the friend?"

*"**FOR YOUR EARS ONLY**"*. A pause followed. "Office of Collection Strategies and Analysis. Deputy Director of Intelligence shop. The number two man. A Mr. Smith. Apparently, they heard about your last interrogation."

Sam tried to explain. "But I didn't do anything. I ...."

"Shutup Sam. The intelligence you gathered might have saved thousands of lives. Maybe even millions. That *ghost* will never be allowed to see the light of day nor speak to anyone but US personnel. If that were to happen, if he were to get out for any reason, you'd be a hunted man."

"My orders then, sir?" Technically, Sam had been on loan to the Other Government Agency since graduation day at Annapolis. Ever since he had showed an amazing aptitude at foreign language, his career had been carefully mapped by others than himself. He still was a commissioned naval officer. Admiral Sauria would one day have a nice sound to it.

This co-mingling of civilian and defense personnel allowed flexibility to the executive branch. It was this methodology that permitted Colonel Oliver North to perjure himself to Congress in a Marine uniform and then be pardoned by Reagan in acknowledgement of his service to country.

"Your orders? To take a thirty day leave. You may have more if desired but thirty is required."

"With this leave, I am to do what, sir?"

"Relax, you dummy." With that retort, "Ol' Hooters" pulled out a desk drawer. The Knob Creek bourbon flowed freely over the next hour as the former classmates enjoyed very fresh Cohibas and shared stories already told dozens of times. There *were* some benefits to being stationed at Guantanamo.

Sam hurried back to his quarters with his two shadows never farther than an arm's length away. Damn, whoever Mr. Smith is, he's serious, thought Sauria. He had direct orders to be off base and relaxing somewhere within 24 hours.

Sam started to pack his gear without any idea where he would head. Wherever it would be it would be somewhere warm. The tropical heat and steady breezes of windward Gitmo were now a necessary part of his surroundings.

Sam dug out a world atlas and started with A's. It didn't take long before he came to a little island by the name of Aruba. A quick game plan came to mind.

Catch a military hop to Miami this afternoon, spend the night carousing South Beach around Collins and Lincoln Avenues, maybe a few minutes watching the chi-chi girls at Mango's contort their well-formed bootys into shapes and motions unimaginable to most humans, and he'd be ready for take-off tomorrow morning for "One Happy Island".

The speed with which Sam finished packing his gear even surprised his self. He hadn't gotten squared away this fast after the 0300h wakeup in Mogadishu. Now all he had to do was relax.

QUEEN BEATRIX AIRPORT, ARUBA

Sam grabbed the first taxi outside the American Airlines terminal and headed in to town.

"Bonbini!" chirped the elderly driver of South Asian Indian descent.

"Bonbini to you, as well." added Sam.

"Your destination, please?"

"Start toward Oranjestad. I need your help, however."

The driver turned north out of the airport and headed up Route 1A. "How may I be of assistance?" Every taxi driver all over the world knew those first two phrases in perfect Queen's English.

"I need a place to stay. Not a hotel or in town but more like a beach villa with maid service and a cook. Not too far from the casinos, as well."

"Oh-Oh-Oh!" yelped the driver sounding like one of the cops on *Car 54, Where are you?* "I know who can help us. You will love it. Just one minute. Yes, just one minute." Barely able to contain himself, the driver began babbling into his cell phone.

The car arrived shortly at a realty office. The driver was greeted as if he were a shipwrecked survivor. The women and men inside poured out to the parking lot and gave hugs all around.

Sam glanced at the name on the license and then the name above the realtor's. They were the same. Sauria chuckled to himself. His driver kept it in the family. A few minutes passed and the cabbie returned.

"Come. Come. I take you to the Gold Coast at Malmok Beach near California Point. Townhouse. Beautiful view. Hotels not far." The little man dropped it in drive and began to leave.

"Wait! Wait! How much? You need a passport and credit card?" Sam had his hand on the man's shoulder.

"No! No worry. I get that from you when you unpack. Sit back and relax. I take care of everything."

Why not, thought Sam. He could afford it. He needed it. An old salt might as well get spoiled. Besides, he had certainly made a new friend today.

"All right then. What's your name?" Sauria extended his hand over the back seat at the first traffic light.

"I am Monbe Chupandilla." He said proudly. "But many visitors, especially the young ones, call me *Chippendale*."

"Chippendale?" Sam smiled broadly. "OK, Chippendale it is" Leave it to Americans to come up with a nonsensical nickname that didn't resemble the person in form or feature because they couldn't remember his name or how to pronounce it, he mused.

"OK, Chippendale. Let's get to the villa. But I want to ask another favor of you. May I have your cell phone number? In case I need something. Snacks, liquor, that sort of thing."

"'Oh sure, sure. Anytime. Just call. You want a tour? I give the best tour on Aruba. The young Americans call it the Chippendale tour. All over. All the beaches. The ostrich farm, the butterfly farm, Hooiberg the mountain, the natural sand bridge......" Monbe carried on like this the remainder of the trip with Sam silently acknowledging him with a nod of his head whenever Chippendale glanced in the mirror.

Twenty minutes later, Chip, as Sam soon began to call him, had Sauria nicely secured in a beautiful townhouse in a gated community with sugar white sand and azure water out his back door.

The man from the CIA was now just another tourist. "Here you go, Chip. Thanks for everything. You got all the paperwork?" Sam handed him a fifty.

"Oh, thank you. Thank you very much. I have everything. Your card and passport will be in the villa when you awake tomorrow. You call me anytime. Chippendale is ready! I have 14 brothers and sisters, all married with children. All in business. You need something, I know someone!"

"All right, Chip. See ya later." Sam had to practically push the overly solicitous driver out the door. Ol' Monbe probably felt like he and his family had hit the lottery.

Sam laid down in the luxurious long-fiber cotton sheets of a king size bed overlooking the Caribbean. The overhead fan on the ceiling and the sea breeze from the open terrace window caressed both his body and his mind. His eyes tracked geckos chasing insects across the wall and ceiling in an ancient game of fox and hare. Neither prey nor predator ever seemed to tire. Sleep came quickly for the first time in many months. The nightmares came as well.

The disturbing images were always the same. Spine rattling screams from faceless bodies then total darkness and the familiar dragging sound of feet on concrete when legs could no longer walk. The sound of a cell door clanging shut perpetually served as the alarm in his head.

Sam sat up. It was dark. He glanced at the clock. 0200h. He had slept away the evening. There was always tomorrow. He rolled back over on to the cool side of the sheet and once more tried to climb in to a gentle place like the comfortable green grass beneath the shade trees of his childhood. He hadn't been there in a longtime in dreams or otherwise.

MALMOK BEACH, NORTHWEST END

Sam returned barely sweating from his morning walk at the beach. Very little change in water height between tides made this beach all the more desirable. A quick shower and some mango with yogurt seemed to do for Sam wonders compared to the Gitmo chow.

He wondered through the open kitchen and opened cupboards and the refrigerator. All were well stocked with local fruits and vegetables fresh from Venezuela. As he scratched his head, an unfamiliar cell phone rang on the counter-top next to which lay all his travel papers along with a well-marked map of Aruba. The phone would not be ignored.

"Hello?" Sam answered tentatively still bewildered about how all these things got in the villa while he was asleep.

"Mr. Sam. It's Chippendale! You ready for island tour!

"I hadn't made any plans. I just want to….."

"It's OK. I'll be there in two minutes. Two minutes only. You like the phone? Good. Look on map. We will go everywhere. Bye."

The phone went dead. Sam laughed to himself. Monbe didn't waste time waiting for responses. The front door swung open even as Sauria laid the phone on the table.

"Hi, Mr. Sam. Chippendale here. You ready?"

Sam's first instinct was to resist this non-stop attack of salesmanship by this modern good-natured pirate but on second thought Sam needed to relax so why not.

"Almost. Be right with you." Sam went upstairs and slipped into a tropical shirt and shorts. The huaraches on his feet felt great compared to boots or shoes.

Chippendale held the door open. "Come on Mr. Sam. We have fun."

The pair piled into the taxi and Monbe had it off and running before Sam could buckle up.

"First we go to California Point....", Chippendale started but Sam interrupted.

"What's up there? I don't want to drive around all day. Chip, I'm trusting you to be square with me. I'm not your average tourist."

"Oh, yes, Mr. Sam. I know this. I saw all the purple ink in your passport. Many interesting places."

Although Sam was using his civilian passport and not the black diplomatic one, it indeed was nearly filled with visa stamps including the unique *Bon Bini an Aruba* most recently. He started to question Monbe about his nosiness but it could easily be explained away by the required registration of his passport number by the rental broker. Sam would wait and see how this played out.

"OK, we're going to California Point. What's up there again?" Sam asked as he started to relax and go with flow.

"It's the most NW point of the island. There's a lighthouse. A wonderful view. If you like to scuba, the wreck of the California is just offshore and down the beach a ways."

"Why does the name sound familiar to me?"

"You might have seen it on TV. There was a big search going on. Some lost girl." Chippendale glanced in the mirror at Sam. Sauria pretended not to notice and made no reaction.

The information carried no significance to a CIA interrogator on vacation.

"Does that happen often? Searches at California Point?"

"Oh no, no, Mr. Sam. It's a beautiful spot and a lover's cove. What did some American tell me one time? The young lovers go to *'watch the submarine races'*. Yes, yes, that was it. The submarine races. You understand Mr. Sam?"

"Yes Chip, I do. It's old slang for parking your car at the beach with your lover. Probably surfer-speak from the '50s."

"Yes, that describes California Point."

"I assume this is California Lighthouse that I see ahead of us?"

"Oh yes, Mr. Sam. Yes, quite beautiful. You agree?"

Looking like the lighthouses found around the world in locales once colonized by the Dutch, its beauty lie in the fact that it overlooked a stretch of sand gone unnoticed save by the local beach cognoscenti.

Sam took a walk around paying special notice to the sea grape groves which were perfect places for a lovers' tryst.

Why would Monbe bring him here at midday? A tidbit he could ponder later.

"OK, Chip. Where to now?"

"I think we go to Bushiribana. We go along Hospitalstraat toward the central windward coast not far from the Natural Bridge. The bridge was carved by winds over centuries of time. Bushiribana is an old gold smelter used by the Dutch"

The drive lasted less than 30 minutes from California Point.

Bushiribana reminded Sam of the underground cities of central Turkey where Christians barricaded themselves against Muslim onslaught. Were we approaching that situation now in large American cities wondered Sam? Is our civilization soon to be fortified by concrete or human barriers? What a great place to hide though, Sam realized. If he needed such a place, he would remember Bushiribana.

Sam snapped a few pictures and urged Chip to leave. He didn't want to appear too interested in this location. As they drove by The Natural Bridge, Sam remembered his time in Utah's Arches National Park. The power of the wind unchained whether it be versus water or rock could not be mollified.

"Now we go the Butterfly Farm and then on to Hooiberg. Big day for us." Chippendale was in the zone as far as being a cab driver.

Sam had had enough. "No thanks, Chip. Take me back to the villa. I'll get changed for the beach and you can take me to one that is more populated. Maybe I can make some new friends."

"Yes, yes, Mr. Sam. Whatever you say. You not hungry yet? My sister and brother-in-law have a wonderful restaurant not far from Eagle Beach. Plenty good Indian food."

"I'm sure they do. Let me change and take me to the beach. That's all I want."

"OK, Mr. Sam." Monbe's shoulders slumped as if he just lost a million dollar deal. Sauria was sure Chip would try again. Good for him, mused Sauria.

Sam was in and out of the villa in no time. All he wanted was a few drinks and a cool breeze. Maybe some conversation about something besides UBL or KSM would help. These six letters were the government acronyms for Osama and Sheikh Mohammed, the two movers and shakers behind 9/11. Sam needed to remind himself to practice not thinking in agency spook speak.

Eagle Beach was only 5K's south of the villa on the main beach road 1A/B. Sam piled out of the back and headed towards the sugar white sand. He waved Chippendale off, but Monbe waved back and turned off the engine. Sam chuckled. Chip was like the guy at a bar one can't get chased off no matter what one says. Sam had a new friend whether he wanted one or not.

Sam wasn't exactly a beach god. Thirty years of long hours, bad food, Turkish cigarettes, and scotch had had the expected effects. Retirement kept circling his brain like sharks in a blood pool. He'd walk a little while in the sun and then find a beach bar. He hoped to lower the blood pressure a little.

As he squeezed his toes in the sand while walking, Sauria tried hard to think of babes 'n bikinis, of which there were no shortage, yet his mind returned relentlessly to old problems. Even the topless women lounging luxuriously in hotel beach chairs, oil and sweat dripping down the anatomical ravines, barely brought joyous thoughts. Screw it, thought Sam. Where's the bar?

He spotted a pier and walked toward it. The electronic steel drum sounds blasting from a tiki bar played out over the playa like Sirens for sailors. The effects were the same.

Sauria settled in comfortably. "So what you got local beer-wise?"

Denys answered as if he had heard the question 100 times in the last hour, treating Sam like another dipso American tourist. "It's Balashi. A pilsener. Brewed locally from our desalinized water. Comes in 700ml cans. You want one?"

"Yeh, sure." What an idiot, thought Sam. Another bartender acting like he is doing you a favor by serving you whines all off-season about being broke. Finding a good bartender was as important to personal happiness as finding a good doctor.

A couple wandered up to the bar but Sam didn't look their way. The view of the white sand and multi-shaded blue waters of the Caribbean were beginning to have the desired affect intended by his superiors.

"Hi, Denys. Back again. How about a couple of Balashis, please?"

The pitch of the voice and the manner of speech shook Sauria from his panoramic daydream. Before his eyes could glance in the direction of the sound, he knew the answer.

It couldn't be but it was indeed a coincidence. He started to acknowledge the couple but he hesitated. There are few unplanned encounters in the spy game. Were they following him? Did they care to play their hands with the cards up as it were? Too late, they decided for him.

"Sam? Sam, is that you? Look Daga! It's Sam!" Wolfe elbowed Daga. She didn't look up. She was finishing her first of what she hoped were many cold ones.

"Denys. I don't suppose this beer comes in a size for mature audiences?" Daga had yet to turn towards Wolfe.

"It doesn't but I do." Denys' demeanor was 180 from how he had waited on Sam.

"Easy hombre. No rude fellas. Remember?" Wolfe would have to keep an eye on this one.

Daga cracked open the fresh one and swiveled to see Wolfe. "Querido, what are 'chu saying? Sam who?" The sun and alcohol at the beach were having the familiar results with Daga.

"Sam from Spain. Sam from New Orleans. Look!"

Sam tilted back his straw fedora and smiled broadly at the pair. "Nice to see you again."

Wolfe started towards Sam and stopped in his tracks. He was having what Sam had already experienced. There are no coincidences.

"Sam, the answer is no. No matter what. We have other business here." Wolfe's face stared back with the look of someone not to be moved from his position of thought.

"It's not what you think, Wolfe. Let's get a bucket of these baby beers and go sit under the coconut palms. I'll tell you all about it." The chance that Wolfe was playing Sam occurred to the long time handler. God, he hated not trusting anyone 100%.

"Don't even try. We would love to sit and talk. That's all? Deal?"

"Deal." answered Sam. He agreed too easily, thought Wolfe.

"No curveballs?" added Wolfe.

"No curveballs, no knuckleballs, not even an Eephus pitch."

"Well, then no Eephus pitch. What the hell is an Eephus pitch?"

"Blooper ball. Drives fast ball hitters crazy. It must be used sparingly like compliments to pretty women."

"Gotcha. Get the beer."

XI

"So Wolfe, what brings you to paradise?" The interrogation had begun. Sam wondered if he would ever have a whole day where he didn't have his guard up.

"Funny, I was going to ask you the same. You know us. Tried and true beach bums."

"But you mentioned business back at the bar. I don't think of this as work unless it's eye exercise. With Daga, you shouldn't need much visual exercise." Sam acknowledged her with a smile and a nod while she fished in the bucket for another beer.

"It's serious, Sam. Completely freelance. We're on our own. It just something that drives me. I haven't even told Daga the whole story, but you first. Why here? You checking up on us or coming to recruit?"

"Neither. Ordered to take a leave. Stress. I was in Cuba. This looked convenient."

"A little too convenient. You sure you're not here to find us? I know you guys are going to keep us on a short leash after New Orleans."

"Sure."

"What happened to make you need a break?"

"It wasn't one thing but a series of things. I'm second guessing my raison d'etre. For the first time in my career, I'm not completely proud of being an American and to be working for the agency."

"Like what? Can you tell me?"

"I shouldn't but I will. Let me refill the bucket. This is going to take awhile."

Sam returned with another bucket and began the dialogue. Daga began another beer.

"As you may have guessed, this is something that has been brewing since before 9/11 but it continues to fester and current events are making it worse." Sam took a gulp of cold beer and continued. It felt good to trust someone. He hoped he wasn't getting duped.

"It's the state of my beloved country and the entire life I've spent in service to it. I don't know if I'm doing the right thing and that thought has never entered my consciousness until recently. Now it does every night and some days."

"Well you know I'm not too happy about what's going on with our government nor am I happy about Americans being killed in cold blood."

"That's the problem, Wolfe. As far as the Muslims are concerned, this is a new Crusade and *we* are the Christian imperialists, the infidels. How much do you know about the Islamic religion?"

"They pray too much and wear funny clothing?"

"Nice try. I know you're not that stupid but most Americans are completely ignorant of the culture and religion of the Middle East. Our government wants it that way."

"How so?"

"For instance. The public has been told ever since UBL bombed our African embassies that the reason is that they don't believe in our decadent culture. Our women are whores and chamber maids whose sole reason on earth is to service our insatiable sexual appetites."

"Don't they cover up their women?"

"But not because they respect them. Because they *don't deserve to be seen.* All one has to do is see what Hussein's two sons did with women to get an idea of the status of females in the Islamic religion. Hell, look at the Taliban. Women were horsewhipped for exposing their face or ankles." Sam swallowed some beer, took a deep breath, and realized he had jumped metaphorically into the pool fully clothed and it was useless to worry about being wet now.

"However, all of that is a smoke screen. The reason they are attacking us is because it is written in the Qur'an that to be a true believer one must attack infidels in a defensive jihad if so ordered by an Imam."

"Defensive jihad? We never attacked them first except for Iraq."

"Wrong. According to the Qu'ran, anytime non-believers occupy Muslim lands a defensive jihad can be called. We have been occupying Muslim lands since the Borbóns and El Cíd chased the Arabs from southern Spain 1200 years ago.

This is the key to UBL. He is very calm and keeps his promises or threats depending on which side you defend. He recruits holy men by basing his arguments on writings from the Qu'ran, therefore couching his war in religious terms. The mullahs and imams then in turn sell the jihad to eager adolescents. Fighting in a defensive jihad to young Muslims is tantamount to taking communion to Catholics. It is required by the writings of Mohammed provided infidels occupy Muslim lands."

"But Saudia Arabia, Quatar, and the Emirates granted us military bases to protect them." Wolfe acknowledged to himself that Sam's discourse was as serpentine as a Casablancan bazaar.

"Remember, Wolfe. These are not my thoughts. But it is reality. When we pre-positioned materiel before the first Iraqi war the true believers were convinced that their holy lands and shrines were being invaded by infidels. It satisfied the requirements for a defensive jihad. As far as the Sunni and Shi'a were interpreting the facts, the royal families are usurpers and squandering the natural wealth of the Caliphates. They sell the oil for less than its worth in order to support the economy of the Crusaders thereby protecting themselves from the wrath of the followers of Allah."

"So if we are there under any circumstances, we are a basis for holy war?" the argument started to sink into Wolfe's consciousness.

"Correct. And we will be there as long as we are sucking on the oil tit. Do you think we would give a shit about the Sunni and Shia blasting each other if there weren't any oil? Hell, we'd let them be like the Darfur region. The next question is why are we still dependent on oil?"

"OK. I give. Why?"

"Because the wealthy elite in America are getting richer on war and oil futures. Bush said 'bring 'em on' after 9/11 and then he kisses the hand of King Abdullah whose kingdom was the source of ¾ of the perps on that fateful day. That doesn't mean Saudia Arabian government officials were in on the plot. It means that there are a high number of radicalized Muslims living in the kingdom who detest the royal family. George W. cozies up to the king because Bush's descendents, from the alcoholic daughters on down, will never have to work nor pay their fair share in social security taxes unless one thinks paying taxes on the first 95,000$ is a fair share for someone whose income will be well into the millions per year.

Middle class sons and daughters are dying so the wealthy industrialists can have cheap oil. It's the Robber Barons all over again. Since Bush has been President the percentage of people in the middle class has shrunk and the number of millionaires and people below the poverty line has increased. When a country loses its middle class, bad things happen."

"The other day a free lance writer asked a gathering of young Republicans about the war in Iraq. They all felt the surge was the right thing to do. Then he asked why they weren't in the military if they believed so strongly. To a person, they all had other objectives on their agenda. Yeh, like keeping their lives, limbs, and inheritances. This is why I'm not sure about what I'm doing."

"What have you been doing?"

"Interrogations at Camp Echo. Guantanamo Bay, Cuba. The worst of the worst or put another way the highest prized detainees that have information that is vital to our security. That is, we get them if the extraordinary rendition program didn't get them first."

"Rendition program? Has the sound of a Nazi extermination euphemism. You know, *relocation,* while we're planning to gas you."

"Well, yeh. Deniability. George W. can say we don't torture. We do, however, deliver people to their tormentors and as a matter of fact we do torture as well. Unfortunately, a certain percentage are innocent and simply swept up in the dragnet. Hell, Cheney invokes the 1% rule. Basically, if we're wrong 99% of the time it's OK as long as we're right 1%. Talk about a low bar requirement."

"But you're not even sure about the Gitmo interrogations?" Wolfe asked.

"Well. That's the crux of the problem. The interrogations have saved lives at the cost of what makes America the stalwart of individual rights and freedoms. The Constitution is in shreds, our troops when captured are dead men walking, yet what I have learned sends my nerves rattling."

"Like what? Should I be worried?" Wolfe glanced over at Daga as she slumbered into an alcoholic dream oblivious to the conversation.

"Where do I begin? Mubtakkar or TWA 800? Might as well go in chronological order. Ever heard of the Bojinka plot?"

"The one about blowing up planes over the Pacific?"

Wolfe leaned forward and set his beer down. It seemed a good time to slow down.

"You got it. 1995. Ramzi Yousef, the first Trade Center bomber in 1993 and his uncle, KSM aka Khalid Sheikh Mohammed, hatched a plot to blow about a dozen planes out of the sky over the Pacific simultaneously while en route to the United Sates."

"Apparently it never came to fruition, right?" asked Wolfe.

"Depends on one's point of view. They needed to check their tactics so they ran a test op. Blew a Japanese engineer out of his seat at 35,000 feet while flying in a 747 from Manila to Tokyo. That of course wasn't the object."

"Killing the guy wasn't the object?"

"Nope. It wasn't an assassination of an individual. It was intended to bring down the plane. But it didn't work perfectly. The pilot made an emergency landing on Taiwan. Those other passengers and crew were extremely lucky."

"So what happened? Why didn't they try again?"

"They did. An alert Filipina police major, inspecting a routine apartment fire recognized bomb making materials. KSM and his nephew escaped capture, Bojinka never materialized, but Yousef remembered his lessons."

"Which were?"

"The bomb needed to be placed so the force was directed downward as it perched hidden under a seat situated above the center fuel tank."

"How they'd get the bomb onboard past security?"

"In pieces. It consisted of a Casio watch as timer, C106D semiconductor, gun cotton, nitroglycerine in toiletry bottles, 9V battery, and a 3V bulb with the filament exposed. All the materials looking perfectly innocuous if packed separately or in electronic devices and personal effects. Once onboard, Ramzi took his toiletry bag to the head, constructed the bomb, placed it under the seat, got off the plane at the intermittent stop in Jakarta, and the device blew over the South China Sea. But not the way he wanted."

"The plane survived. He wanted to blow the fuel tanks?"

"Exactly. So our FBI is let in on this little secret by a savvy Filipino colonel in their intelligence service and basically we sit on our hands."

"Now fast forward a couple years. Yousef has been apprehended in Pakistan through bribery and is awaiting trial in NYC for the first Trade Center bombing. The FBI gets the bright idea of allowing Ramzi to call back home real time, no tape or broadcast delay, to see if they can listen in and pickup some intelligence. Trouble is, Yousef throws them a curveball and speaks a tribal dialect used sparsely in NE Pakistan. The FBI can't find an interpreter because they can't even ID it so they don't record it, and before you know it, while Ramzi is on trial in Manhattan, TWA 800 blows up near Moriches Inlet from a center fuel tank explosion. You tell me.

Hell, it so closely resembled what happened to the Japanese engineer and the captured designs in Manila it nearly caused the judge to declare a mistrial while considering a defense motion to that effect because of the prejudicial repercussions on the jury."

"So why is that making you wonder about yourself and your life's work?" seemed like an obvious question to Wolfe. Meanwhile, the sun was down, so was Daga, and planets were beating a path ahead of the soon to appear stars in the night sky.

"Because the intelligence community denies, denies, denies. You know the rule. Deny, deny again, deny louder; never stop denying. I sent an aardwolf assessment through my Chief of Station on this matter. The ambassador cannot edit it. It goes straight to the DCI. Nothing.

There are several wonderful investigative reporters and writers that have piecemealed this together but the majority of their brethren just repeat the party line coming out of the White House Briefing Room. Meanwhile, I'm sworn to secrecy."

"Someday Sam, you'll be proven correct."

"Wolfe! I'm subject to federal prison for what I've told you so far. Get it?"

"What about this mubtakkar thing? Didn't that work out?"

"Same thing. Depends how you look at it. Is it OK to torture people if one gets information that saves lives? How many? What type of torture? To the death? I don't even know those answers."

"You did the torturing?" Wolfe reached for the last beer, popped it open, and slammed it in a single gulp.

"Of course not. But if an American intelligence officer witnesses torture, and does nothing to stop it, yet gains invaluable information, is he guilty of a war crime or is he a war hero?"

"What type of torture?"

"Oh, Wolfe. You can't be going there? You mean there are degrees? You mean you can kinda torture someone or kinda rape them?"

"For example?" Wolfe was glad that Daga was passed out but he needed some more beer. Denys noticed the empty bucket and read Wolfe's mind.

"Well, let's see." Sam struck a pose like a college professor pondering a student query. "Our personnel have used the following techniques with the SecDef's consent, according to senior commanders commending interrogators for their good work."

"Sleep deprivation, sensory overload with lights and sound, sensory deprivation, humiliation through nakedness, nakedness in the presence of females, extreme cold to the point of hypothermia sometimes resulting in death, and dogs. Hard to prove murder when someone dies of being cold. You just warm the body back up and ship it to the morgue. An excellent pathologist will catch it, but it's not like our people are looking that close."

"Navy SEAL's will tell you the hardest part of training is the hypothermia. But these techniques are only for the run of the mill insurgents. The high value targets get a free ride on the rendition express. Then it gets serious. The Egyptians and Jordanians do a pretty good job along with the Bulgarians with their Romanian henchmen.

It's how we learned about "the invention" mubtakkar. We didn't get all of the details because the prisoner died but he put us on the right path. Later on we got the minutiae at Gitmo. Remember the elevated terrorism warnings in NYC and the additional beat cops checking back packs and briefcases at subway entrances? That came from torturing people."

"What did the detainee die of?"

"Hard to say. Like I said, the autopsies where these guys were being held aren't that thorough. Could have been drowning from water boarding, heart attack from electric shock, or traumatic shock from seeing your left ear held in front of your own eyes and then tossed to a dog for a snack. Anything is possible. Those black glove dudes are pretty imaginative."

"I'm beginning to see your predicament."

"You catch on pretty quick Wolfe but even I don't understand it and I'm in it. Then on top of it all, I'm awarded a CIA commendation and medal for the NYC deal. Of course, no one will ever see it, it's held in a secure location at Langley and it may never leave the building. Whoopee!"

The beer had finally gotten to Sam. Between the alcohol and the release of all he had held inside himself, exhaustion won out.

"Sam, time to go." Wolfe looked up and there was Chippendale smiling broadly.

"It's OK. I take Mr. Sam home. I take care of him."

Wolfe would have none of that deal. "I'll go with you. It's late and we need a ride as well. You can drop us last." Wolfe glanced over at Daga and shook his head. Even passed out she was beautiful.

"I see the lady is tired, too. No problem." another good day for ol' Monbe.

The drive to Sam's place at Malmok Beach and then back to the marina gave Wolfe time to think about all that Sauria had said. Sam slept on the way to the villa while Daga snuggled out to the world in the crook of Wolfe's arm. The sky filled with twinkling lights and the warm, salt breeze wafted in the taxi windows.

Tomorrow would come and Sam would want to know why Wolfe and Daga were in Aruba. Should he tell him the truth? Could he tell him the truth? Sleep might bring the answer.

XII

The morning brought the usual perfect weather to the "A" island. Wolfe rolled out of the berth, made some coffee, and found his favorite spot on deck near the bow. Daga wouldn't be stirring for awhile.

A good night's rest had performed as he had hoped, his mind made up, Wolfe got the feeling of satisfaction that washes over one when a decision has been made and now all that remained were the planning and action phases. The mulling of options often became the most difficult portion of any enterprise to be considered.

Moaning sounds and bare feet slapping the deck announced Daga's awakening. The word chipper did not come to mind when confronting her after a night of drinking.

"Good Morning, watermelon head. How you doin'?"

"Silencio! It hurts when you talk." Daga held up her palm in the universal stop sign. Wolfe started laughing. Daga made a face. "What's so funny?"

"You mean it hurts when you talk. It doesn't hurt when I talk."

"No. I mean it hurts when you talk. Shut up!"

Wolfe wouldn't give up that easily. "Apparently, the baby beers were large enough."

"It's so funny when I'm the one hurting. Why? Why do you always laugh?"

"Because you remind me of Lucille Ball. A famous comedienne from the 50's and 60's. Every once in awhile she'd do a drunk scene and it left one in stitches. You act just like her when you're hung over."

"Stitches? What 'chu mean *stitches*?"

Jesus. She's still drunk, thought Wolfe. "It means you make me laugh."

"We'll see who's laughing when you sleep on deck tonight."

"Whatever. Nice try. If you behave at the beach today, I'll give in tonight. Go below and get changed. We're going to find Sam." Wolfe bit his lip holding back more chuckles.

An assortment of clatter, patter, crashes, and thumps drifted above deck giving Wolfe even more entertainment as he imagined her hopping on one foot while putting on her sandals or throwing things looking for her bathing suit. All of this usually took awhile. He settled back into his spot.

Eventually, she emerged ready for the beach looking considerably better. As the pair descended the gangplank, a familiar voice spoke up.

"Hello, Mr. Wolfie. Sam sent me. We're headed back to the beach." Chippendale never missed a fare.

"Oh, are we now?" How do you know?" Daga glared at Chip as if he screamed in her ear. He actually took a step backward.

"So sorry, miss. Sam said you would come. Besides," a broad smile crossed his face, "you're dressed for it." However, the grin left his face when Daga continued to stare. He took it as a signal to open the passenger door, gesture at Daga to sit, and wink at Wolfe as he closed the door for them.

"Sam didn't say what he wanted?"

"No sir, Mr. Wolfie. Only to come and retrieve you."

"Well I hope it's Eagle Beach. That's where we're going."

"Yes sir. Sam said that's where you'd want to go. He's already there."

"Why didn't I know that?" a small smirk on his face acknowledging what was obvious. Wolfe settled in for the ride while Daga held her head in her hands and tried to keep it from moving. The periodic squeaks and groans indicated those times she found herself unsuccessful.

Sam greeted his old friends with a bucket of Balashi. Daga turned her head and almost barfed. Wolfe laughed and popped one open.

"Hey, mate." Sam tried out his badly effected Aussie accent. "It's your turn today."

"My turn? I don't mind buying if that's what you're saying."

"It's not buying you'll be doing. Talking is what I need."

"Come on Sam. How much of what you told me, was true?"

'Too much. Make sure to buy a pencil from me if you see me on a street corner. I need you to tell me why you're here on Aruba. To soothe my doubts."

"Always cynical?"

"Comes with the job. Being sardonic keeps one alive doing dangerous things."

"I see. You don't trust me?"

"More than most. Does that count? I've already trusted you with my freedom."

"On purpose?"

"On purpose."

"Fair enough. Where do I begin?"

Before Sam could respond, Daga stretched out on the beach, put on her IPOD, and blocked the world from her consciousness.

"I don't know. I know a little about you because of your dossier. That's it."

"Tell you what. Tell me what you know and I'll pick up where you leave off."

"Fine. Here we go."

"Take your time. Don't leave anything out. Have a beer before you start."

Sam cracked a beer and began. "This is what we know and I emphasize the *we*. You're a baby boomer, excellent test scores, athlete, haven't trusted the government or authority since JFK, can't be bullied either at work or on the field, counter-suggestive and passive aggressive. Your parents were uneducated but passed on good genes. You're not model handsome nor Frankenstein ugly. You're an extreme extrovert with useless information but you never allow anyone, female or male, to be close except for a few lucky or unlucky ones depending on one's point of view. You believe that you may have perhaps a handful of real friends which is accurate. Even those you mislead harmlessly. Never cross you. You defend the underdog. You absorb information when exposed. How am I doing?"

"You can stop now. What color were my grandmothers' eyes."

'The Cherokee had brown and the Frenchy had green. Satisfied?"

"My eyes?"

"If you insist. Blue in moderate light, gray at dusk or dawn, green in bright light and out of doors. One uncle has one blue eye and one green eye."

"You win. I'll start with just before our paths crossed. As you said, I don't trust the government and based on your situation I'm feeling pretty good about it. Your agency recruited me for New Orleans because I'm also a patriot but not an ideologue. I cried like a baby on 9/11 yet did not suffer personally in the loss. I'm here to take care of a bully."

"A bully? You've been in a fight?"

"No-o-o-o. But a bully is anyone who takes advantage of weakness and especially vulnerability. In this case, it's by drugging someone. I'm on the trail of what I think is a sexual predator and murderer of young women. Which brings me to this. I want your help if what you told me last night is true. The kid is rich, his father is powerful, but he has soft spots where he doesn't know he has them. You in?"

"Doesn't sound like much of a vacation?"

"It's not, but compared to what you've been doing it could be very satisfying."

"I'm sure he deserves it. Brief me up to speed."

Daga rolled over, joined the group, and Wolfe revealed both the history of his prey and the basic plan.

"Some of this is only conjecture so we'll have to play it by ear depending on how the chips fall. Literally. If he wins, it makes our job more difficult. Based on what I've seen, he has a better chance of growing a third hand then winning in a casino.

The more he loses the more likely he is to fall into a familiar pattern of behavior in order to bail out. This is where we come in the picture. Once you see him in action, Sam, you'll have no doubts about what you're doing."

"I'd like see and hear a little more. I'm going to take some time and do research and gather some materials. Maybe tweek your plan a little. Perhaps call in a couple markers from old associates. Can't have too many options. See you two tonight at the Bonita Beach Casino?"

"That's it. He'll be there most likely. Maybe with the two yahoos if we're lucky. You'll get a good chance to see what I mean."

"OK. You guys enjoy the beach. Daga, try not to cause any heart attacks in old men or embarrassing moments for young ones."

"Don't worry, Sam. I'll be more likely to skip a beat before anybody else does. You know, closer to the fire." Wolfe was only half-joking.

"If he keeps laughing at me when I'm hung over, he may live forever." Daga cut her eyes at Wolfe. She wasn't joking.

Sam made his farewells and on cue Chippendale showed up as if he were watching from the tree line which was probably the case. "Where to now, Mr. Sam?"

"Back to the villa, Chip. Vacation's over."

"You leaving the Happy Island? So soon?" ol' Monbe looked absolutely depressed.

"No, Chip. Change of plans. Don't worry. I'll still need you."

"Oh that's good, Mr. Sam. Very good."

Sam and Chippendale drove off as Wolfe and Daga made it a day at the beach.

"OK, Wolfe? What am I going to do?"

"You're going to do what you always do. If we need you to kill them, entrap them, defend me, or intimidate them then that's what you do. Capisce?"

"Capisce?"

"It's Italiano. Entiendes? You understand?'

"Si.si. I understand. But once you let loose my dark side it can not easily be recalled."

"That's exactly what we need."

Back from the beach, Wolfe and Daga prepared for the evening of sizing up their prey. Daga modeled her dress for Wolfe.

"What do you think? You like?"

"Sure. Why don't you just go naked? Why is it that the less cloth used in a woman's outfit, the more expensive the garment?"

"Are we a little *celeso*? Jealous, mi querido?"

"*We* aren't anything. I thought you might want to blend in a little more this evening."

"Don't worry. He'll figure me for another stupid mujer. To him, all women are slow."

Daga had a point. The young Kuiper would only see her as another possible victim although a little older than the naïve lambs. Wolfe had to admit she was stunning regardless of what she wore so the outfit really didn't matter. He took the time to admire the dress as she finished in the mirror.

The fact the garment was a single color the shade of spring wine in Tuscany made it unusual. The body inside of it made it unique and possibly a new wonder of the modern world. Starting above her right shoulder, it hung loosely in gathered rows across her chest alternating between cloth and skin until the forces of the body within it seemed to smooth the cloth as it became one with her hips ending in a handkerchief hem mid-leg. The slit running from above the curve of the left hip to the selvage trimmed in rosé only added intrigue to the stunning view which Daga accepted as her burden in life.

"You look great, baby. Sorry, you're with me." Wolfe had on black and black. It wouldn't matter what he wore. If Daga were in the room, everything else was secondary.

"Ready? Let's go." The pair negotiated the steps to the upper deck gingerly and arrived in the refreshing breeze that whipped the island without falling. Evening clothes, especially for women, are not made for sailing the high seas. What now was becoming part of the local ambience chirped up from a perch on the stern.

"Oh, you look very nice indeed, Ms. Daga. Mr. Wolfie a lucky man. Yes?" Chippendale hopped down to the deck positioning his self at the gangway to assist Daga.

"Don't tell me. Sam sent you." Wolfe negotiated the descent to the pier himself.

"Yes, yes. He's already at the casino. I think Mr. Sam needs some help with how to wear clothing. His tuxedo does not fit."

"He'll survive. Tally-ho Chip." Ol' Monbe drove off while Wolfe chuckled to himself. He might as well laugh before he got serious.

XIII

The casino hopped with excitement. When Daga came in the front door, her entré didn't have a prayer to make it any less so. Wolfe spotted Sam immediately upon entering. While most eyes went to Daga, Wolfe glanced at Sam.

From a seat at the video bar, Sam's mouth moved endlessly as he burned the ears off a female bartender. Sauria wore a classic Armani black tie ensemble but Chip was right. The inseam was too long, his shoes looked like they had been polished with dark chocolate, and his tie pointed to the magnetic pole and not East and West.

Sam acknowledged Wolfe's presence with a nonchalant glimpse as if he were surveying tonight's losers. Rebelle would lead and Sam would follow. The target was in plain view.

Kuiper sat at first base at a blackjack table. This would be easy. Sam previously, and now Wolfe, spotted the two males who served as Dirk's cleaner fish, hanging nearby and enjoying the natural security like clownfish in a sea anemone. They weren't so far away that the protector couldn't be reached in an emergency yet ready and willing for any leftovers from their royal patron.

"Hey. It's you again. Hi, Dirk. Remember, I'm Wolfe?" Always the first to do so, the American extended his hand. Rebelle settled into third base.

"Oh, hello. Just got here myself. Need some luck."

"Don't we all," added Wolfe. Kuiper seemed a little more human. Relaxed attitude is a characteristic of someone whose had made up one's mind. Sam slid into seat five playing the role of a drunk American.

"Hey! How ya'll doin'?' The words were barely out of Sam's mouth before he bent at the waist rather than bring the cocktail to his mouth. He slurped louder than a little leaguer at a ball game with a dog and a soda.

The dealer started the shoe and the games began. Wolfe and Sam bet the 25$ table minimum while Dirk chased bad money with good money. He displayed the classic loser's MO. It was Sam's play that twisted the knife.

After losing the third hand in succession, the kid couldn't be quiet any longer. His anger was directed at Sam.

"What the hell are you doing? The dealer had a 7 showing and you had 14! You didn't take a card."

"Hey, man. I didn't want to bust."

"Well that's fucked up."

"We try not to talk like that where I'm from. You play your cards and I'll play mine."

"You're playing for 25$ and I'm playing for 500$?!"

"Yeh, I wouldn't play for that much." Sam slurped from his drink.

Kuiper literally exploded. "Where's Klaus? I need more money!" The dealer unfortunately happened to be the closest target of Dirk's anger.

The same dance duet that Wolfe had seen a few days earlier accompanied by the same steps played out between Kuiper and the burly pit boss. First the gentle discouragement to continue play presented and then the acquiescence to the loan request. This kid won't ever get it. It made a perfect confluence of events.

An hour later the original threesome strolled from the casino with Chip waiting like a loyal lap dog. The conversation in Ol' Monbe's back seat was lively.

"You saw his play, right Sam?"

"If you want to call it that. He's terrible. What'd he drop tonight, 25G?"

"Something like that."

"Well, we know it's not his allowance."

"Exactly. How'd your homework turnout?" Wolfe knew Sam hadn't been sitting at home idle.

"Uno momento! You don't want to know about the two hangers-on?" Daga interjected.

"We already know. If you were blond, they would have been all over you." Wolfe responded.

"Don't worry, Daga. I've already got plans for them. Actually, they won't get off easy. Trust me." A countenance that Wolfe had never seen crossed Sam's face when Sauria spoke those words without any show of emotion.

Wolfe was afraid to ask exactly what Sam meant because he knew it wouldn't be useful to know. As far he or the objects of Sauria's plans were concerned, some people are too good at what they do. Wolfe preferred ignorance and Sam granted it.

Had Chippendale been able to read the minds of his passengers, this pleasant little man would have stopped the taxi and gotten out and ran.

Instead, the bringers of justice sat quietly in the back seat, each keeping his or her own counsel, planning what very few could ever imagine and certainly never do.

A few miles away the targets had very little conscience and never a moment of conscious foreboding. For most of the conspirators, the countless nights of restful sleep in their lives, now had a finite number.

XIV

PUNTA DE GALLINAS, COLOMBIA
SUDAMERICA

Peninsula de Guajira, the rainforest

The fortress, to call it a house or mansion would be to ignore the 8 foot thick walls of reinforced concrete, sat deep inside the rainforest of Colombia's NE coast at elevation. An hour drive from wide open beaches, the cargo could be imported from Aruba and the other islands with a brief 80 mile boat ride. Using go-fast Danzis, the freight could be in Aruba at midnight and inside the stronghold by 0200h.

When the DEA and CIA started killing and capturing most of the narco-traffickers after the invasion of Panama some of the younger generation switched business plans. There was other contraband to be smuggled. Nearly as profitable, this operation existed well below the radar of the Americans.

Kuiper drove the bow of the boat to a soft landing in the deep sand. The lanterns, made of coconut shells and hanging from trees, resembled shrunken heads from a bad Tarzan movie. Easily seen from sea, the soft glow guided his passage to the rendezvous.

Four-wheel drive vehicle headlamps flashed on and the sounds and silhouettes of men moving toward him were easily heard and seen. He hoped he could do this less often. He had learned his lesson. No more would he harvest from large groups. Too many people were aware of the missing. He'd keep to solo flyers only.

"Is she alive?" one of the men, obviously the leader, asked as he reached the boat.

"Of course, what good would she be other wise?" Dirk hated these people but the money was great.

"Is she what el jefe ordered?"

"She is beautiful, young, blond, and what I could get. A yellowtail."

"For this much money, I hope she lasts longer than the last one. She had no tolerance for drugs. We only got one month out of her. Bad genes, huh?"

"No idea. Jefe still made money. Let's get going." Kuiper shrugged his shoulders and stared at the leader who motioned with his hand.

The waiting men scrambled over the gunwales. Wrestling with the body which Dirk had wrapped in blankets and tied with rope, they got it on their shoulders and eventually to land. Only a quiet moan escaped the package.

"Here is your money. You'll be back?" the leader handed over the paper bag of 100$ bills US.

"Sure, sure. Contact me as always through the DJ." As long as he didn't get desperate for money, he could take his time and not be under so much pressure. He would let the DJ scout for targets and then decide if he wanted to risk it.

Kuiper, with the help of the leader, pushed the bow of the Danzi back into shallow water while the kid jumped on board. The deep baritone of the inboard engines signaled his departure. He'd be back in bed in 90 minutes.

If there were any questions asked, his parents would swear he'd never left the house. As far as they knew, he had gone to his separate bungalow at 2330h. He nestled the bag full of blood money under the console and gunned the engines. The cool salt air blew through his long blond locks and stung his face. His former passenger's ride wouldn't be nearly as nice nor end as well.

CASA CONCHA, the fortress

The living quarters of the building were decorated in typical poor taste reflective of unsophisticated people who find their way to large sums of disposable income. Oversized furniture, gold and diamond chandeliers, and wine-colored draperies running from the 18ft ceiling to the floor were not in short supply. The walls were painted in art deco pink both outside and inside however unlikely it was that the owner had chosen that color only through happenstance.

Hand-carved ebony shutters framed both the windows and the view below from atop the mountain. Paintings of garish female nudes, only one level above Elvis velvet art in depicting the painter's skill or the human aesthetic, hung throughout the room. White Italian marble graced the floor with South American emeralds centered within each tile.

Armed men packing Hechler & Koch MP5 closed bolt automatic machine guns seemed equally spaced throughout the main salon and open veranda. Positioned Twenty-five meters apart, the guards had at their convenience 40 caliber Barettas for additional firepower. The weapons laid about like candy dishes or conversation pieces.

The object of the guards and the weaponry lounged shirtless in white cotton pants. A gaudy gold chain and pendant hung from his neck entangled in wiry black hair. The gilded necklace contrasted greatly with the swarthy skin made even darker by hours at the pool. Nevertheless, at this point in time, his pants were around his ankles while one of the chicas, still free to roam the grounds, kept him *occupied.*

His name was Angel "Chulo" Ayala. The pimp. He thought of only one thing most days and all he did and owned reflected the obsession. The name of the fortress, La Concha, literally translated to *the seashell.* However, in South American slang it referred to the female genitalia. Such was the level of his one-mindedness.

As if perfect timing were his birth right, the chica finished her work as the leader of the beach patrol entered the room. He waited silently, averting his eyes, as Chulo adjusted himself.

"You have her? Is she what I wanted? She didn't die enroute did she? You better hope not. I'll hang your cojones from the doorknocker. She cost me 100,000$ US."

"She is in good shape but very drugged. She is as you wished. I will place her with the others unless you would like to see her now, El Jefe." No one called him Chulo to his face except for his peers and business associates.

"No, no. I'll wait. I don't want to spoil the moment."

Angel turned on his heels and left the room. That motion announced the end of the conversation and signaled the patrol leader to make his way to the entrance of the cells with his men in tow and carrying the package.

The holding cells were for new arrivals and used *goods*. This dungeon was easily accessed through the underground entrance to the motor pool. They looked like tiny one room apartments if one didn't notice that all of the women were handcuffed to the walls.

In the middle of each cell there stood a padded bench, elevated in the middle, so as to accommodate a single body in the same manner as an S&M spanking apparatus. At the foot of each bench were more loops spiked to the floor. The metal had been perfectly positioned to restrain a victim's arms and legs. One manacled in such a way would be headfirst bent over with one's legs spread eagle.

Chulo had thought of everything. Medical personnel were present to take care of bothersome STD's and to administer the heroin which kept the captives helpless. The women in these cells had been exhausted by Ayala and his business associates and were now earning the profit margin for which they had been purchased.

The prices for these chicas were similar to used cars. The newest arrivals were 200$ while the prices declined to 2$ for those with precious few days to live before a final trip to the rainforest. The prices were based on fifteen minute increments.

There were some other cost differentials. Yellowtails tripled the posted price and were kept longer past what would have been acceptable. To be a yellowtail, one's curtains had to match the carpet.

The girls living in the fortress per se had it much better; for a while. They were free to roam about the grounds and house but to be on call and ready to work within fifteen minutes. In extremus, it could be an evil version of the Playboy

Mansion out of control and administered by a psychopath rather than a kindly grandfather.

The prices for these women were considerably higher but not so lofty that wealthy businessmen and Arab oil royalty didn't fly in from all over the world to allow themselves the unspoken pleasures they couldn't get at home. To tycoons, 5000$ a night or 10,000$ a weekend amounted to a hand or two of Baccarat.

Blondes increased the cost accordingly and reconstructed virgins were available on a one time basis of 250,000$ for reenactments of Aztec sacrificial ceremonies after no longer qualifying for the real show. When Angel bored of them and their talents they were shipped to the cells below.

Such was how Angel "Chulo' Ayala made his living and how Dirk Kuiper earned his gambling stakes.

These two men and their criminal activities were indicative of the order of life in the third world. Something the travel brochures with beautiful pictures of beaches and exotic places never bother to explain.

Males, foreign males, farm animals, pet animals, and local women, in order from most to least social value, occupied the first five tiers of the hierarchy. Foreign females managed to come in sixth just one position above the bottom tier; unescorted foreign females hanging in bars at night.

It is something Americans don't grasp so well. You're not in Kansas anymore. Beware of the smile. Human life is greatly devalued. If something happens to you, it will have little or no effect on the lives of the locals.

There is an exception to this rule. Cruise ship passengers are given a free pass because to victimize people with loads of money to spend and only a short while to do so would affect everyone's income. However, when the sun dips below the horizon, the home team has the advantage.

This deadly game of Darwinian existence snatched up millions worldwide and hundreds of Americans each year. The problem with the Americans is they didn't know they were in the game. Even the few who suspected as much, didn't realize the stakes. The police could always be called to save them. Unfortunately for most, the referees didn't like the visiting team.

XV

Chip dropped all three musketeers at Sam's villa after a stop at a liquor store which was closed after hours but conveniently owned by a Monbe relative. There was a premium added to the price but that is the cost of doing business in the Caribbean.

"OK. Where do I begin? There's a couple criminal enterprises operating in around this Kuiper kid's sphere of influence." Sam cracked the first bottle of Pusser's rum. Daga immediately became more interested.

"Start wherever. We're really only interested in Kuiper." Wolfe gulped the sweet liquid of the cane and glanced over his glass at Sauria.

"Not that easy. Firstly, the casino is run by a criminal enterprise out of Marseille. The sole purpose of which is to launder drug money from *ecstasy*, sometimes called X, manufactured in the Netherlands and sold mostly in Western Europe and the USA."

"What's that have to do with the slimeball? He's not using X, he's using something like GHB!"

"Because the guy that has the kid hooked for money, Klaus Bruin, is the soldier for the Marseille Syndicate as well. The more money the kid loses, the easier it is to launder the other money. We don't want in the middle."

"OK. Fair enough. Where's the kid getting the cash? Wolfe slurped down some of the cold liquid. Daga made them both another drink.

"That's where it gets interesting. Couple of friends I have in the DEA told me they have pulled over a go-fast boat every few months coming off Colombia headed to Aruba. Picked it up on AWACS look-down radar. Figured it was running drugs. Want to guess who's driving?"

"Kuiper. What'd they find?"

"Nothing. Zero. Zilch. Nada. After awhile, the boys figured the kid had a little side sweetie over there and could afford to go see her. That's when I got to thinking."

Sam held up his empty glass to Daga, and she filled all three glasses with the rest of the first bottle.

"What? That he takes the drugged girls over there? Makes sense."

"Yeh, but not to bury them. To sell them. That's where the money comes from."

"Anyway to find out where?" This Dirk dirtbag was worst than Wolfe thought. Hard to imagine.

"I have a telephone appointment with an old acquaintance of mine. When I get done with her, if she knows anything, we'll know it."

"What makes you think she does?"

"Remember the cocaine wars of the 80's down in Miami? Murder Capital USA. 600 homicides per year related to drug trafficking. The media concentrated on the Colombians.

They were the importers. It was the Cubans who distributed and did the enforcing. The head of that snake was a female. The Godmother of Cocaine. The Black Widow. The DEA has her on a string. Nothing happens without her getting the scuttlebutt. She'll talk. She has no choice. We have her stashed in Colombia. It's safer for her there. Can you believe it?"

"Let me know. Daga and I will start casing the other two. Right now, let's finish the rum."

"Rum will make you dumb! Si? And caliente tambien. How 'chu say? Hor-nee?" Daga hadn't wasted any time not drinking.

Wolfe shook his head. "Sam may we stay the night? I've got some work to do."

'Tough life. How do you manage?"

'It's not easy being me." Wolfe swept Daga off her feet into his arms as she had begun to disrobe. Sandals and a thong eventually littered the steps.

Sam stayed on the couch and dreamed of ways to do this op right.

Near 0500h local time, Sam dialed the secure satellite phone number that could only be traced by the NSA. The federal bodyguard answered and handed it to Griselda Blanco, formerly known as The Godmother of Cocaine, but now answering to Federal Protected Witness #199,845. She had been the most prolific killer in Miami during the drug wars but Blanco had never pulled a trigger.

"Griselda. That you?"

"Sammy. 'Chu sound good."

"How do I know it's you?"

"Double café cubano on calle ocho."

"I need some information."

"I know. You don't call me for love. Only business."

"What can I say? You were always the smart one."

"Who is it this time?"

"Who's running a white slavery/prostitution ring between Aruba and Chicken Point? Anybody we know?"

"Sure. Has been for years. Chulo Ayala. I hate his ass. Wish he had come to Miami in the 80's."

"He was only 15 then, Griselda."

"Old enough to die." Griselda had earned her nicknames by total disregard for innocent bystanders, children, and possible witnesses with the emphasis on the word possible.

"Where's he held up?" Sam waited. The very talkative Blanco suddenly turned laconic. "Come on Griselda, it's part of your deal." Sam urged.

"You play hard, Sammy. Muy difícile."

"You can always check–in to the Colorado Supermax."

"Si, si, si. I know." She brushed her graying hair from her face in a sign of resignation. "He's in a fortress an hour's drive inland from Punta de Gallina. Gross income approaches 100$ million per year. Heavily guarded. One way in and out. Buries the leftovers in the rain forest."

"Thank you, Griselda. I'll call you again if I need you."

"I wished you lived in Miami in the '80's."

"That's the point, Señora Blanco. I wouldn't have been living."

XVI

The next day Chip shuttled Wolfe and Daga back to the boat and then just as quickly left to get Sam. The threesome met in downtown Oranjestad at an outside bar across from the cruise port.

"Three Balashis, please," ordered Sam. Daga held up her hand. "Don't worry girl, I'll drink it if you don't. What's a matter, the rum isn't playing nice?"

"It's like an evil lover. You like it when you're together, but the next day not so much." Daga held her head in both hands.

"OK, Sam. What do you know?" Wolfe interjected.

Sam told of his conversation with Blanco and then began to lay out the plan.

"We need some pictures of these yahoos. Once we have those, we've got a connection with the local police chief. He'll identify where and when they can be found besides in the casinos. We have to trail them for a few days."

"Once you start nosing around, won't the cop spill the beans? These are local kids. Wealthy and powerful, in the case of Kuiper." Wolfe wanted nothing to go wrong. His blood was up even more since Sam had described the money-making portion of Kuiper's crimes.

"He'll try his best not to do so for his own sake. The chief is taking money from the narcos. We turned him quite awhile ago. He's scared to death. We let him keep the money as long he keeps the information flowing. He doesn't want to end up as Noriega's cellmate, or worse, with a Colombian necktie and his balls wrapped around his head. He won't like it but so what."

"Fair enough. What's our assignment?"

"Well, it's more like Daga's. You can tag along but she'll have an easier time getting what we want. Besides, she can kick their ass if they screw up and try something. Daga, you get close to them. Figure their daily routine. I want you to become part of the everyday scenery. How you do it is up to you."

"We'll think of something. I'm looking forward to getting these wild dogs."

"Fine. So far, nobody knows what we're doing. Once we talk to the cop, we'll have to start taking counter measures. He may let it slip out to his wife or girlfriend because he *is* scared. It goes down hill from there. Here's my local cell number. I'll get the two of you a couple of those pre-paid disposables. I figure we roll up the first part of this in a couple of days. Happy hunting."

Sam scooted his chair from the table and shuffled with one shoe untied back to the street where Ol' Monbe waited like a loyal servant with a driver's license.

A few hours later while Daga and Wolfe grabbed some rays topside at the boat, Chip pulled up to the dock. Sam wasn't with him.

Now Chippendale was a good driver but his eyes went directly to Daga as she laid splayed on the deck facedown. Her bikini top dangled from the mizzenmast in a Caribbean version of the Dance of the Seven Veils. It took all of Ol'Monbe's self-control to bring his eyes to Wolfe.

"Mr. Wolfie. Sam sent me." Chip handed Wolfe a package. "He said to open it right away." Chippendale scurried from the deck like a cockroach when the light is turned on.

Wolfe tore open the package. Inside were two cells and a sheet of paper with a few scribbles. Before Wolfe could read it, one of the cell phones rang. The ring tone electronically beeped out the notes to "Shock and Scandal", a winning Calypso song from carnival years ago. It was one of Wolfe's favorites.

"Hello, Sam. What's with the ring tone?"

"Thought you'd like it. If somebody hears it, you'll seem more like an ex-pat than a tourist."

"Always thinking. What's on the sheet?"

"Operational intel. Read and light a cigar with it."

"Will do. Talk to you later." Wolfe flipped the phone shut and placed the second one next to Daga's ear. He called the number Sam had given him. Her phone rang with the notes from "Big Bamboo." Sam still had a sense of humor. Daga didn't budge.

When Daga finally awoke a few hours later grumpy and still hung over, Wolfe was half-way through a bottle of Cruzan dark rum.

"Get cleaned up, my lovely. We got work to do. Hurry before I get drunk."

Shortly, the two were in Ol'Monbe's taxi headed to Playa Linda Casino for some gambling and a little pre-op intel.

Twelve klicks away in a small café, Sam settled in across from the police chief.

"That was a pleasant phone conversation we had today, Chief. Did you find out what you needed to know?"

"I'm not here for conversation. You checked out. Tell me what you want. Quickly. I answer. Then I leave. You're goin' get me killed. Start."

"Come on, Chief. This is supposed to look like a social call."

"I don't have social calls from Americans. That's ridiculous."

"That obvious, huh? Anybody asks, tell them it's an interview from a big American newspaper. Travel editor. Wanting to know how safe Aruba is for Americans. Tell whoever is asking that you gave the usual standard line from the Tourism Bureau. Simple."

"Enough. What do you need to know?"

"I'm going to bring you some pictures in a couple of days. I want names, addresses, cell phone numbers, any peculiarities. Where they work and where they play. Got it? Don't leave out important information that may be helpful to me because I may have failed to ask for it. It is your responsibility. I get a surprise, you get a surprise. Understood?"

"You want these people for what reason?"

"Now that's not any of your business, is it? Down the road, I'm going to want you to inform your men that if they wander across my path to look the other way. No accidental interference of my op. Is all of this clear?"

"Very."

Sam stood and shook the Chief's hand while smiling widely. "Remember. Journalist for tourism."

Wolfe and Daga entered the casino at Playa Linda. Wolfe wore his Jimmy Buffet runway ensemble complete with linen pants and huaraches. Daga displayed her wares with the help of blue jeans and a white linen shirt tied at the waist. The snowy cloth contrasted beautifully with her café au lait skin while her blue eyes glimmered like diamond bits. Even when she dressed down, she effected men all over the world the same.

Both Wolfe and Daga were armed with disposable cameras. It was time to play tourist. Wolfe headed to the blackjack pit and Daga to the adjoining bar.

Their targets were already in place with the addition of a fourth.

The pit boss or pit bull, depending on one's point of view, greeted Rebelle first. Klaas practiced his best insincere smile. "Hello, Wolfe. How are you this evening?"

"I'll let you know in a couple of hours." The American returned the affected smile and added a similar handshake. The pair had performed the accepted social dance among opponents in a casino. It amounted to the non-verbal *it's just business* among men of a certain type.

Dirk Kuiper sat at third base. This time he greeted Wolfe. "I see you like this game as much as I do."

"I only wish the feeling was mutual. You know, if the game liked me as much as I liked the game. Most times I feel like an unrequited lover."

"A what?"

"Unrequited lover. One's passion for a woman, or in this case a game, is not returned in kind."

"Oh, I see. Yes, I have that problem with the game. Never with women."

"I'm sure." It's hard to be turned down when the female is drugged into a coma, thought Wolfe.

Daga was having her own success at her location after a slow start. Within minutes of sitting unaccompanied at the bar, she chased away a few drunk would-be suitors. They weren't the fish for which she waited. The three man crew hanging at the end of the bar didn't hesitate after the last rebuff. They knew they had the right rap.

Arriving carrying a rum and coke for Daga, the three young men surrounded her, confident in their game. If only, they knew. Daga swung her stool around to face them, chuckled and entered the contest.

"Senorita, you are quite beautiful. What is your name?" The man speaking was Anthony "Tony T" Traficante. He earned a living being a small time drug dealer and DJ.

"Mine is Daga. What's yours?"

"Oooh. Daga. That's an interesting name. Is that your real name?"

"No. My real name is Dagmar. Just some of my ex-boyfriends thought I was good at making a point. Now what's your name?"

"Tony T. These are my friends Hoeboe and Hoepoe Chowan." Daga recognized the pair from the other night; the ones of South Asian descent. This new player was Latino.

Daga settled into an evening of drinking and harmless flirting. Before the party went their separate ways, Daga got a photo of each with her.

Daga headed out to the main casino to see how Wolfe was doing.

For once, the Dutch kid actually won. Certainly only this winning night, out of four or five losing ones, would remain in his memory. Bad gamblers notoriously remember only the good days.

"Who's this one?" Dirk directed his gaze at Daga as she approached while he colored up his chips.

"She's mine." Wolfe used the crude third world version of *she's with me* to signal possible beaus that she had male company. It made her sound as if she belonged to Wolfe as property. To many males in that part of the world, she fell into the category of chattel.

"Lucky man." Some of Kuiper's snake oil salesman personality slipped through the cracks of his façade.

"I think so. Where you heading now?"

"Downtown. You and your date want to come along?"

"We'll pass. However, we'd love to have a photograph of the three of us and maybe one of you and Daga before we leave. You know, for a souvenir."

"Sure. Daga and I go first." Dirk positioned Daga in front of him and while Wolfe prepared the camera pinched Daga's ass.

If he had known what she was thinking, he would have visualized his intestines splayed on the floor while he dreamed of a quicker death. Instead she smiled over her shoulder and told him that in spite of Wolfe's pleasant personality, he did succumb to jealous rages which usually resulted in someone dying. The smile disappeared from her face and she turned her head back to Rebelle. Kuiper blew through the stop sign and put his hand back on her hip. Daga signaled Wolfe with her eyes.

"Hey Dirk! Cut it with my girl. She's worse than me. Trust me."

Kuiper eventually took the hint. "She's hard to resist." Once rebuffed, the Dutch kid began planning what he thought would be his pleasure and Daga's demise with out realizing he had traipsed into a one-way ticket to hell.

Wolfe and Daga left with what they had intended and Dirk left with something he would never achieve.

Daga steamed all the way home. "Leave him for me, Wolfe. That little pendejo grabbed my ass. Next time I'll give him a reminder he won't be able to forget."

"Easy, baby. We don't want to put him on guard. He'll get his. If we can make it happen, you can do the honors. Satisfied?"

"OK. But I'm not satisfied. When we get to the boat, I'll be satisfied." Daga warmed up Wolfe on the ride back to the marina. Chippendale hung his hat on the rearview mirror. Otherwise, driving safely would have been impossible.

XVII

Two days later, Sam settled into a chair at what was becoming a familiar location. The Chief arrived shortly thereafter, right on time if one followed Caribbean appointment protocol. Anywhere between the hours counted as the previous hour. 1459h qualified as 1400h. Sauria passed the photos across.

If the Chief were a poker player or a car salesman, it wouldn't have mattered. His face was a road map of disaster. It's not a good thing in either game.

"These are the people in whom you are interested?"

"They are. Is there a problem?"

"No problem to ID them. Problem is what happens when I do."

"It won't be as big a problem then if you don't."

The Chief's Adam's apple bobbed up and down a few times, he swallowed hard and began. "The Chowan boys. Hoeboe and Hoepoe. Work at a computer store downtown on Smith Boulevard. Between the two of them they are there all day. The tall blond one is a little more difficult. He's the son of a judge. Name is Kuiper, Dirk. Lives in a cottage at his parents' house. No visible means of support other than his wealthy parents. Seems to do pretty well with the tourist girls. The Latino is Tony T. Local DJ on a boat that cruises the nearby waters while the passengers party."

"You got addresses?"

"I've got addresses. Don't cause trouble that can't be explained. I don't need it."

"Don't worry. They're about to be winners of an all expense paid trip."

"What?"

"Just do what you're supposed to do. No questions."

Sam excused himself and went to the bathroom, when he returned, the Chief had made his exit as planned.

CASA CONCHA

She awoke in a fog. She had no awareness of her whereabouts nor time and space. She tried to roll over to her stomach but something kept her right arm trapped. She passed out.

What may have been minutes or hours she did not know but she awakened again. This time the murkiness of her consciousness was not as severe. She sat up. Her eyes strained to make out walls and a floor. This time she noticed the chains and manacles that held her right hand to the wall.

Voices in the distance were more than just a rumble. The high pitched sounds of females but not in English would be her guess. Words were interspersed with quiet whimpers and howls of horror. The bars at the end of the bed came in to focus. Her heart sat squarely in her throat beating uncontrollably while thumping a deafening rhythm in her head.

She lay back down and passed between more or less periods of awareness. She heard metal on metal and became keenly aware that someone had opened the cell door. Forcing herself upright rapidly, she huddled in the corner of her bed forcing her knees to her chest.

A strange man stood at the foot of her mattress; staring. He had Latino features, moderate height, and pitch black hair. He wore white cotton pants with a guayabera unbuttoned to his abdomen. Multiple gold chains and medallions hanging from his thin neck completed the unintentional caricature. His smile reminded her of the greasy used car salesmen on local TV commercials. His words came to her in what seemed to be slow motion.

"Hello. I am An-gel." He pronounced it in Spanish. "In English, you would say Angel. So that is good. You can call me Angel. I am your Angel."

"Where am I? Who are you?" Judy Miller, blond haired, blue eyed farmer's daughter from Ohio was becoming hysterical. She struggled against her constraints. All the years of volleyball and cheerleading had never prepared her for this moment. Bible school never mentioned places such as this or the men like the one who stood relaxed in front of her waiting for her to realize what had happened.

"Please, tranquilo. Calm down. It is of no use. I will tell you everything. First, however, you must understand your situation."

"I want to go home."

"You will never go home. The time you spend here can or can not be very luxurious. It is your choice. However, you will never go home."

"My parents love me. They will look for me. We have money. You can't get away with this."

"With what? I've been doing this for years. They don't have a chance. But enough of this, allow me to tell you what your situation is at this time."

"I can pay."

"You already said that. They can't pay enough. Now be quiet."

Chulo began his usual introduction to hell on earth. "You have been kidnapped and then sold. I purchased you. You're currently recovering from a heavy dose of GHB. Your friend Dirk administered it to you in a drink. I tell you this because it doesn't..... it is of no concern to me. The reason of my purpose is I own you as a sex slave; first for my pleasures and then for anyone willing to pay."

Judy Miller had strong bones and better genes. She couldn't keep from shaking.

Her down home upbringing made her wish she would soon wake from a bad dream.

"Con permiso, with your permission, I will explain to you your options and then you may decide how you will spend your time here."

"I will never do what you want. You can kill me."

"I don't need your permission to kill you. You need my permission to live. The question is how you live. I can tell you that many come here with the same attitude as you in the beginning. Shall we say, they often change their point of view.

No more useless words. It wouldn't be fair for you to decide without a tour. Guardias!"

Chulo snapped his fingers and two guards appeared. One gagged Judy Miller while the second one chained her feet and then her hands to a constraining belt. They pulled the crying, whimpering woman child to her feet.

"First we will show you what will become of you if you decide not to cooperate. We prefer cooperation but we can handle whatever."

The group turned down a second corridor. Men were standing in line. Each had coins and currency from all over the hemisphere in his fist. None held an amount worth over 2$. They were campesinos and trabajadores; field workers and laborers. Ayala stopped the tour at the front of line.

"This is where you will be if you fail to comply with my wishes. It is as always your choice."

A shabby curtain hung in front of the cell door. It did not hide all nor was it intended to do so. The woman or what was left of her was bent over the padded bench naked and spread eagle. Her hands and feet cuffed to the floor. One campesino finished and another took his place. The hapless female never moved. For lack of better words, she had achieved lifelessness before the actual state of being.

"So far this is the fate you have chosen. Uncooperative women come here. They never leave walking." Angel stared into the terrified eyes of his captive. "Now I will show you how you may live, if you choose."

Up a set of stairs on to the main living level, Judith Miller shuffled her feet. Magnificent doors the height of the ceiling opened to expose what well could have been a modern version of a harem.

Females of every race and shape lounged luxuriously on thick sofas and cushions. Big screen TV's played entertainment of choice. A large pool and spa occupied considerable space while women reposed mindless of the new arrival. Judith Miller realized it for what it was; a velvet cage.

Tropical fruit bowls decorated tables full of beverages of every sort. Massage tables stood against the walls occupied by beautiful women receiving warm oil massages from Asian females.

"You may live like this or you may live downstairs. It is completely your option." Chulo snatched the gag from Miller's mouth. Of course, what he didn't tell her was that all eventually ended up in the cells; either from overuse, age, or simply to make space.

Judith knew she had to decide. She would never make it out alive from the cells. She had a chance from here. She begged for God's forgiveness for what she was about to do.

"I see I was mistaken. This doesn't look so bad." She did her best to affect the mannerisms of the ditsy blonde he expected her to be.

"Unchain her." The guards complied. "You will be taken to your room where you will find all that you will need. You will have an attendant to bathe you and provide any unforeseen needs. You will be delivered to my salon when I am ready."

As he finished speaking, a matronly older woman came over and guided Judith Miller away to her new life as a sex slave.

Judith Miller, straight "A" student, bible school attendee, camp counselor, and cheerleader was kidnapped for sexual purposes on her first trip out of the country. She had to go to college, get married, have children and grandchildren. She fainted on the way to her apartment.

The matron helped her back to her feet. "It's OK, chica. An-gel treats us well. It is a good life. You will see. Vamos. We will make you pretty again."

Judith Miller shuffled her feet to regain her balance. The American struggled to walk down the hallway. The matron shook her head. How many times in the past had she given that little speech? She acknowledged to herself that all must do what it took to survive. This was her lot in life.

XVIII

CIA RENDITION PROGRAM, S.E. ROMANIA

Here they played for keeps. Guantanamo seemed like the minor leagues. The Ivy League boys that still inhabit the intelligence community have, in many instances, extreme senses of humor, or more accurately, love the ironic twist of fate.

The free world press, the International Red Cross, the United Nations, and Amnesty International would never find these detainees. Solzhenitshyn's gulag seemed like child's play.

Vlad the Impaler had inhabited this place. Over 3000 Turks had been skewered on the sharpened trees outside this fortress. Its name is Poenari. The methods of the real Dracula would have been less painful for the captives. They were stuck with Romanians who were working for the CIA although that information never seemed to be said. The locals enjoyed the work.

Most detainees were here because it was thought they might know the whereabouts of Osama and other high profile targets. Therefore, they know and would tell, or not know, lie, and then die later.

In parades eerily identical, guards and prisoners entered the lower level of the castle and heard the screams emanating from the ancient dungeons. There were a few prisoners who looked American.

One man stood out among the others. The master torturer had come to this line of work honestly. He had honed his skills first for the Soviets and their puppet Nicolae Ceausescu. Later, he switched sides after the execution of the dictator and his wife. Men who did what he did well were always needed on the winning side.

His nom de guerre, Kpobb, meant blood in Russian. The CIA boys managed to make it K-Bob. The Master prepared for the first treatment of what he hoped would be a long day.

This particular prisoner had been captured outside Kabul while burying roadside an Explosively Formed Projectile. A more deadly type of ambush device than the IED, it was one of the pleasant new Iranian designs passed on to Al Qaeda to help kill Americans more efficiently.

When initiated by microwave transmission, molten copper formed from the explosion and then was literally shaped into a penetrating projectile aimed at the underside of the vehicle or the driver's door. These new bombs turned even armored Humvees into flattened boxes full of spare body parts. FEMA trailers wouldn't have done worse. The Americans wanted to know how and when the Iranians got the EFP to Afghanistan.

K-Bob opened the freezer door. The prisoner hung naked from meat hooks inserted in the loose flesh above either side of his clavicle. The blood seeping from the wounds had frozen in red rivers of ice but hemorrhaging to death was not the object of the exercise.

The first indications of hypothermia had long since passed. The prisoner approached unconsciousness and shortly thereafter death. K-Bob wouldn't let that happen. Rapid demise had no entertainment value for those who do this kind of work.

The object of torture is to reassure the prisoner that only the right information will save him. If the captive thinks that death is inevitable, no valuable facts will be forthcoming. The tormentor causes him to believe that the possibility of survival exists. Death only comes as a necessary consequence either by over-aggressive techniques or the requirement of no living witnesses.

The guards hoisted the man down onto a gurney and medical personnel quickly began the core warming required to save his life. Warm IV's and humid oxygen at normal body temperature were administered in an attempt to influence the brain stem into returning the body to its stable metabolic processes. His handlers wanted to bring the detainee back to life; for a while.

The Master would go enjoy his breakfast while he awaited sufficient recovery to begin his work. This part of the exercise reminded him of the practice of putting alcohol on the needle entry point during a lethal injection. The result would eventually be the same.

While the morning passed and he bided his time, The Master checked up on his apprentices who were busy doing the early work on what would become his artful canvasses of pain.

The learning curve for tormenting someone was steep. Sometimes the eager assistants would kill the prisoner before important information could be gathered. This batch of henchmen was coming along nicely.

He stopped to peer inside an interrogation cell to measure progress with a new arrival. K-Bob would have asked the hapless soul a question but he was currently being water-boarded.

Water-boarding could be done in a variety of ways but always with the same objective; to terrify the victim with the near death experience of almost drowning. This torture method produced enhanced outcomes with those who happened to be terrified of water while trying to swim on top of it.

The acolyte had chosen the procedure where one is strapped on one's back to a board inverted at a forty-five degree angle. The prisoner's face is covered with a wet cloth and then gallons of water are poured over his mouth for extended periods of time much greater than the amount of seconds one can hold one's breath.

Aspirating a small amount of water, "going down the wrong pipe," is something with which most people can associate. Gallons of water is called torture. Too many gallons is called drowning.

They used local river water so if an autopsy were done the flora and fauna found in the alveoli of the lungs matched the organisms in the water where some hapless hiker found the body.

Finished with his tour, The Master headed back to his melting prisoner who had finally warmed to the point he could mumble answers to the questions or nod his head.

K-Bob entered the room. His victim was strung by the thumbs at a height which required the prisoner to carry his weight on his toes. When the calf muscles soon tired then the entire mass of his body dangled from the thumbs.

"Good evening. I trust you find the conditions here a little more to your liking. Let us begin." He waited for the translator to change his words to Arabic. No response was forthcoming from the hanging body. The defrosted flesh would soon begin to feel the pain again of the meat hook wounds. "No matter." A wave of his hand dismissively signaled to the prisoner his lowly status.

It took awhile but soon the detainee began to respond in a last ditch effort to save his life. It, of course, was never a possibility. Americans might leave witnesses, Romanians don't.

"I received materials and training from VEVAK in camps in the Dashte Kavir."

"How did you come to be outside of Kabul?"

"The Islamic Revolutionary Guard Corps guided me during my infiltration from the Pakistani tribal areas through the Hindu Kush."

"How were you able to cross the border without detection by Pakistani security?"

"The ISI has many sympathizers for the Taliban. The mosques and madrassas schools maintain their influence over the people from birth to death. If as adults they join the intelligence service, their true loyalty remains with their religious leaders."

Kpobb had heard enough. He ordered the guards and translator out of the room. The remainder of the day would be spent on the torturer's entertainment. Today he thought he might use the hammer. The skill came in not breaking any bones. Soft tissue decomposed rapidly.

When finished, the body would be put back in the freezer until death and disposed of in the surrounding mountains. People get lost in the woods and die of hypothermia regularly. The animals would do the rest.

First thing next morning the Company boys on site in a nearby town received the transcript of the detainee's interview.

The choice of the word *interview* continued in the best traditions of Orwellian euphemisms. Most of what the Americans read they already knew. This prisoner only corroborated many others.

"Same ol' shit. The Iranians are conducting a war against us with their proxies and we can't respond. It's the same reason UBL got away in the first place way back in 1998. We had to ask over flight permission for our cruise missiles from the Pakistanis. By the time our surprise package arrived, he was long gone, warned by the ISI."

"All we can do is, continue to collect proof. We're not the warriors or the policy makers."

The two CIA men were at least confident in one aspect of their task. They would never be prosecuted. The reason the Americans received the information in this manner achieved the all important concept of *plausible deniability*. If anything ever came to pass and they found themselves testifying to Congress or attached to a lie detector, they could accurately say they had never seen any torture, nor evidence of torture, and certainly had never participated.

The questions asked by committee members were often comical to operatives trained in deception. Over the years many top intelligence officials had mislead Congress but never had they lied. The distinction was an important one. Perjury could be prosecuted. The art of deceiving congressmen fell under the heading of well-trained.

It amazed those who did testify that a legislative body crawling with attorneys and charged with over sight could ask such ambiguous questions. The open-ended inquiries and nonsense answers were likely a sum of incompetence and collusion.

Critics and cynics described the proceedings as resembling induction ceremonies for secret societies. Everything classified in the hearings as Top Secret would soon be leaked to the press. Everything actually classified at the top levels of secrecy would never be mentioned nor found in the committee minutes.

This game had been played for so long by both parties they sometimes forgot the rules. One thing remained constant. If one read about a top secret government program in the newspaper, it never was top secret.

XIX

Ol'Monbe dropped Sam at Eagle Beach. He soon found Wolfe and Daga lounging languidly as if recovering from a tough night with the rum bottle. Somehow too much juice of the cane couldn't even cause the voodoo priestess to look anything but stunning.

"Good morning." Sam greeted the pair. He wore the same oversized and wrinkled Bermuda shorts with a Hawaiian print shirt he had worn in their previous meeting. His footwear were the usual combination of fashion faux pas one could expect from Sauria; open sandals with black socks. The prerequisite straw fedora lay tilted back on his head.

"How'd you make out with the Chief?"

"Fine. There'll be no interference from him or his men."

"When do we start?" Daga was eager. Putting together the Griselda Blanco information and her time with the scum bags in the casino gave her all she needed to be self-motivated.

"Tonight. Tony T is working the party boat. Looks like his last shift."

"Do we grab them all at the same time or what?'

"Nah. One at a time. Let the others start wondering. A little bit of panic goes a long way. Be down by the cruise port around 2200h.The party boats pushes off about 2230h."

"Will do." Wolfe and Daga made their goodbyes. Sam shuffled off toward his waiting taxi and self-appointed chauffeur.

The Falo Fiesta lay tied at the dock. Two decks, one was open topside, and the other closed below, provided plenty of space for drunken tourists and locals to mingle. Multi-colored electric party lanterns shaped as seashells were strung bow to stern along each gunwale. At least the Arubans appreciated the significance of the name of the boat and the form of the lights.

Tony T had the speakers blaring rap and club reggae as Wolfe and Daga purchased their tickets at the nearby kiosk. One could purchase drinks on board but the price of the ticket included free rum punch as well.

Up the steep gangway the pair walked. So far, neither had seen Sam. Wolfe got the two of them a glass of punch.

"Mi Dio. Wolfe, you taste this drink?" Daga held her glass at arms length examining it as if it were a poisonous potion.

"Not yet. Why?"

"Try it. Tastes more like 151 than anything else. Why do you suppose that is?"

"It's not against the law. The tourist girls get drunk faster and the local boys have a higher batting average. Keeps them selling tickets." Wolfe sipped the drink. Even the grenadine couldn't hide the alcohol taste. "Keep watching, Daga. The Americans will be slamming the punch and the locals may have only a small social amount in order to make an entré with a girl. They've been playing this game a long time."

"Where's Tony T?"

"Sounds like below decks. Let's go check it out."

Daga and Wolfe made their way down a level on an open metal stairway. As they hit the dance deck, Sam's silhouette came into view. He glanced over his shoulder to see them approaching.

"What d'ya think?" Sauria swept his hand across a 180 degree view of the party.

"Looks like a bunch of drunks to me. Where's Tony T?"

"Back at the stern hiding behind the outcroppings of speakers and amplifiers. Probably getting a hand job from that hot chick next to him. Did you see that cheesy sign he has on the front of the bandstand?"

"No. What's it say?" Wolfe couldn't read it from his position.

"I can't believe he has it. It reads 'no requests but I can read lips'. The scary part is it works. Since I've been standing here at least two girls have disappeared below the turntables."

"So this is our guy tonight?" Daga had a forward lean like a distance runner at the starting line.

"Yeh, we'll get him when they return to the dock. He's not going to like it."

"What do you have planned for him?" Daga wanted to make sure he got what he deserved.

"Don't worry, Daga. Couple of days from now he'll wish he had never met Dirk Kuiper."

USS HAWAII SSN 776

OFF THE COAST OF ARUBA

"SEAL Team 2 away, sir."

"Very well. Maintain night surface running. What's the ETA of the op boys back at the boat?"

"Thirty minutes each way. Single package extraction."

"Very well. As you were, chief. Contact me in my quarters when we 're ready to set sail with all aboard."

"Aye, Aye, sir."

The Chief of the boat swung his binoculars back toward the beach. Wonder what this guy did for us to come get him tonight, he thought.

The Falo Fiesta nestled up to the dock in downtown Oranjestad. The drunks struggled mightily with the inclined gangway. One or two of them took a heads first tumble. Sam gave the instructions.

"You two just play back up in case I need it. Hang down by the dock. I'm going to lure him with money."

Tony T emerged from behind his equipment with a girl on his arm. Sauria intercepted the pair.

"How you doing? I'm Sam. May we speak privately?" Sauria glanced at the girl.

"What about? Who are you?" Traficante looked bewildered.

"I told you, I'm Sam. El Jefe sent me." Sauria glanced at the girl again.

Tony finally got it. "Honey, go on over to Carlos and Charlie's. I'll be there in a few minutes." Traficante gently pushed her in the direction of the gangway. Then he turned and faced Sam.

"What's this all about?"

"Money. What else?" Sauria was reading Tony's eyes. They were unsteady and darted quickly from side to side. Sam couldn't tell if T didn't buy the story so far or was under the influence of drugs.

"We've never done it like this and I've never seen you before."

"Yeh, change of plans. I'm just following orders. The money's stashed up at Divi Beach. Usual amount. You just need to come get it. A little birdie told me that Dirk could really use his share. You don't want to be the one that tells him you didn't think the cash was important." Sam relied on greed to close the deal. Most humans rarely disappointed his expectations when it came to money.

"OK, let's go. I've got to get back to the party."

Sauria and the DJ disembarked and headed for Chippendale's waiting taxi. Wolfe and Daga melted back into the crowd.

"Where to, Mr. Sam?"

"Divi Beach."

"Oh, that's close. No problem. My cousin has a restaurant there…."

"Chip. We're not hungry. When you drop us off, come back for us in fifteen minutes. Now please drive."

Ol'Monbe shut up in spite of the difficulty to do so. Wonder why Mr. Sam so uptight, he thought to himself. He stopped the taxi at the beach access and the two of them walked through the line of sea grape trees out to the stretch of sand.

"OK, let's get this over with. Where's the money?"

"This way down the beach. Behind a tree." Sam put Tony on the side nearest the surf as they walked.

Tony T never saw them coming. Out of the breakers two men approached the DJ silently from behind. His first realization of something gone a miss was the sharp stinging sensation in his neck as one of the men delivered the quick acting sedative by injection. The other SEAL *gagged, bagged and tagged him*, placing a hood over his head and plastic cuffs on his wrists after first taping his mouth with all purpose duct tape.

They turned and addressed Sam. "That is all, sir?"

"That is all. Carry on. Give him a nice ride."

"Will do, sir." The SEALS hustled the body over to where the 30 foot Ridged Inflatable Boat(RIB) lie camouflaged by palm fronds. DJ Tony T Traficante was on his way to Gitmo.

Chippendale returned exactly in fifteen minutes. Sam got in the car.

"Where's the other fellow?"

"He decided to hang with some girl he knew."

"He knows lots of girls. I see him with different girl all the time."

"Take me back to the villa, Chip. I'm tired."

"Yes, yes, Mr. Sam."

EAGLE BEACH, 1200h

Daga lie topless back in the tree line where the sun managed to sprinkle a few spots not shaded by the coconut palms with bright UV's. It had taken Wolfe a few minutes to persuade Daga to be a little more discreet if she insisted upon getting sun on her boobs at the busiest tourist beach.

Sauria ambled up almost as if he knew exactly where to find them. Daga rolled on to her stomach. Not for her benefit as one might suspect, but for Sam's. She wanted him to be able to think.

"How's everybody?"

"We're fine. How did it go with the scumbag." Wolfe sensed by Daga's body language that Tony had made out considerably better dealing with Sam than with Daga.

"He's on his way to Guantanamo."

"How did you manage that? He doesn't exactly fit the profile."

"Neither did Jose Padilla. I told them that he laundered money for drug cartels and that I suspected the cash eventually ended up in unregistered Muslim charities. That'll keep him busy for awhile. By the time they let him go, he won't remember how he got there."

"Three more to go." Daga seemed more relaxed after Sam's briefing.

"Remind me not to get on your bad side." Wolfe added.

"I figured the DJ was some kind of lookout. If he saw something interesting, he gave Kuiper a call. Kirk is too smart to leave much of a trail. We get rid of Tony and Kuiper may get desperate. Especially if he keeps gambling the way he does."

"What do we have planned for the brothers?" Wolfe could imagine even as he asked the question.

"Well, they have more guilt. Best as I can tell. Traficante took a cut of the money. He was greedy. The brothers took a cut of the flesh. More like turkey buzzards than money hawks."

"Let's hike up to the bar and get some Balashis. Daga put your top on underneath your cover up before I have to get in a fight with some idiot bartender."

Oh, Wolfie. You're no fun." Daga did her best pouting face and voice.

"I'll take care of you later. Don't worry. Come on, Sam" The two men walked a few steps ahead of the voodoo temptress.

"How do you do it?" Sam looked over his shoulder to make sure Daga was still behind them.

"Do what?"

"Deal with her peculiarities, let's say. How do you hang on?"

"I don't, Sam. I ride and ride and then I get thrown off and I get back on. Just like breaking a beautiful mustang. Eventually it begins to trust you and you get thrown off less often. You still get bucked from time to time. It's never a smooth ride but always worth the effort. Honestly, if Daga were a flavor, she'd be delicious."

"It certainly seems so."

Denys was at his usual spot behind the bar. He glanced up to see Wolfe and Sam approaching. He didn't move from his seat on the cooler until Daga came into view.

"Bucket of Balashis, please." Wolfe yelled as the threesome took their seats.

"Sure. The three of you have been on our island quite awhile. Most tourists only stay maybe a week. Why so long?" Denys set the bucket of beer in front of them.

"We're considering moving here. The weather is nice. Why not?" Wolfe didn't like the question. Bad vibes began bubbling in his mind.

"When we see the same face for a long time and it doesn't belong to a native, we start thinking Christopher Colón. Are you developers?"

"No, no. Nothing like it. Old friends trying to find a spot to relax. Why? Shouldn't we?" The bubbling increased its intensity.

"Shouldn't you what?"

"Consider moving here."

Denys settled onto the edge of his cooler like a school teacher at his desk settling in for a lengthy explanation to the class. The instructor began the lecture after first filling the bucket with more beer.

"Aruba is a funny place. We're very happy here. Perfect weather. Very few hurricanes. Mostly just tropical storms. We only tolerate the tourists long enough to take their money. We need the visitors but we certainly don't want them to stay. Trying to buy property here is nearly impossible for a non-citizen. International corporations have difficulty without setting up a subsidiary in Aruba to be the de facto owner. Everyone knows everyone like a small town in America.

I don't believe you would like it here." Denys stared at Wolfe. Neither man looked away.

"Thanks for the info." interjected Sam. "We're probably going to stay here a few more weeks. Do some more gambling."

"Ah, poker players? It is becoming very popular here."

"We like it some times. I personally love to call a bluff. Very exhilarating." Sauria was doing the interrogation tango.

"What happens when your opponent actually has the cards?"

"Doesn't happen very often with me." Sam flipped some money on the bar and motioned for Daga and Wolfe to follow. "Have a happy day."

When the group reached a point beyond the hearing of the bartender, Wolfe started with the questions.

"Did we just get warned away?"

"Sure sounded like it to me. He must get paid as part of the ring. Scouting for talent, keeping his eyes and ears open. Bartending is perfect for that sort of thing."

"Do we look that obvious?" asked Daga.

"You don't. We do. Especially me. Wolfe can blend a little when you're around. These guys are naturally paranoid. Wait till Tony T doesn't show up for work tonight. It'll get worse. It's as he said. We're on their turf. The Chief could let something slip, Chippendale might be babbling away at a family dinner, who knows.

The gambling story will give us a couple of weeks. Hope that'll do it."

"They don't suspect why we are here, do they? How could they?" Wolfe began running all he had done since being on the island through his memory.

"They don't have any idea why we are here. They figure what ever it is, it's not good. Probably think we are DEA. They're hoping to nose around and make us aware of them asking questions in order to make us think our cover is blown. We need to act as if we have nothing to hide. We don't want to start behaving like the proverbial duck. You know, if it walks like a duck, quacks like a ......"

"Like a duck, then it's a duck. I know." Wolfe interjected.

"The racket they're running is not the run of the mill criminal enterprise American agents pursue or even imagine exists. These yahoos are just being cautious. New faces aren't good when you're a criminal."

"So how do we get to them?"

"They'll let their guard down. We need to surveil them without being obvious. It helps that this is a small island and not a big city. Seeing the same faces more than once in a single day while in public is not unusual here.

I'll do downtown and you two do the clubs and casinos. It won't be that difficult. If you think you're being made, break off the surveillance without leaving. If you jump up every time a suspicious person enters, then you're acting like a duck. Cops like to go in to clubs just to see who scampers out the door. Got it?"

"No problem. Keep us posted. See ya around."

Wolfe and Daga walked back to the secluded area. Sam had Chip take him back to the villa.

"Hello, Mr. Green, or White, or whatever." The Chief of Police greeted Sam at the door. Sam's advanced skills as an operative were about to be tested. Years of training and practice allowed Sauria to keep his "poker face of no concern" gently in its place.

"Bonbini, Chief. How are you today? Maybe you should welcome me, since you're in my residence."

"Enter and close the door. I have questions."

"Questions? You have questions, Chief? What kind of questions? Like how long you'll be in an American prison for drug racketeering and money laundering? Those kind of questions?" This was high stakes poker, and as such, aggression paid off.

"Well, I mean...."

"Look Chief. Let me explain. We own you. We either own you inside prison or outside prison. Currently you are outside. Are you complaining about the arrangements?"

"His mother came to the station. I've known her since school."

"Whose mother?"

"Traficante's. What can I tell her?"

"Make up something. Say you saw him with an American girl at the airport. They seemed to be in love. She dressed in expensive clothing. Tony was just being a tomcat out on the prowl. You know how young men can be. He'll be back."

"She won't drop it."

"Rather ironic..."

"What?"

"Nothing. Do your best. If you fail, say goodbye to the island. Now leave and never come here again unless you're leaving the program and throwing yourself on the mercy of the court."

"I'll never do that. I'd rather..."

"Eat your gun? Fine. Go for it. Whatever you do, stay clear of my lane. Adios, pardner."

Sam walked away and as he did he heard the door close softly behind him. Sauria hoped the Chief had laid down his cards.

JOINT TASK FORCE HQ– GITMO

"Tell me again why he is here?" Admiral "Hooters" Huck wasn't a pleasant man with whom to deal when confronted with outrageous information by ambush.

The *biscuit*, in Gitmo speak, waited to compose his words carefully. The doctor was one of the shrinks on the Behavioral Science Consultation Team that gave advice to interrogators. In a perfect example of the twisted world of military acronyms, biscuit became his job title. He was attempting to explain the happenstance of a new arrival; from Aruba.

He began again. "His folder says he is a money launderer for illegal Muslim charities. That's how he got here. But when we ran all of his preliminary psychologicals and interviews we got conflicting information. He claims to be a DJ in Aruba.

He knows nothing about Al Qaeda. Even passed a lie detector test with no deception.

I think he somehow just got caught up in the net."

"IN THE NET?!! THERE'S NO FUCKING 'NET' IN ARUBA!! ARE YOU FUCKING CRAZY, TOO?!"

The Admiral reached in his drawer anticipating the comforting effects of the Kentucky corn mash. He tried to compose himself. He filled the glass three fingers deep, contemplated the situation, and then drank the brown liquid down in one gulp.

"Doctor, you're dismissed. Hold him with the juveniles at Camp Iguana as long as he's no threat." The psychiatrist scrambled for the door.

'Hooters' Huck poured himself another bourbon. This portended a hunk of bad luck. How would he ever explain why a detainee was actually a DJ from Aruba?

The realization swam over him much like the warming feeling of his Knob Creek whiskey. Didn't Sauria go to Aruba?

When his fist hit the desk, the bottle of bourbon wobbled as if it had imbibed too much of its own spirits.

"GUNNEY! GUNNEY! GET IN HERE!"

The door swung open to the office and an unfortunate gunnery sergeant stood sweating profusely in 68 degree air conditioning.

"Get Sam Sauria on the phone. He is somewhere in Aruba. I want him as of yesterday. Is that clear?!"

"Aye, aye sir." The gunney about-faced and exited the presence of the Admiral. Like many enlisted men when finding themselves the immediate target of an enraged senior officer, he replied in the positive before ever considering how he might fulfill the actual order. The trick was to get out of range of the verbal shelling and then consider one's options.

XX

Judy Miller had lost track of time. The days blended quickly into one another at Casa Concha. The daily routine consisted of lounging around while nibbling on delicious tropical fruits in a scene reminiscent of the glory days of Rome. Periodically, one of the girls would be picked by a visiting businessman and disappear for a day or never be seen again. Unknown to the women, this depended on the buyer's twisted fantasy.

The other females soon accepted the new girl's presence and the social mingling began in earnest. This was the intended method of capture-bonding utilized by Chulo. Angel Ayala was many things most of which were wrapped in a web of wickedness and evil but no one who knew the master pimp ever thought of him as stupid.

Judy Miller, blonde hair and blue-eyed innocent, became a victim of her own evolutionary psychology. Chulo knew just how to play the human mind of a captive.

Miller was being admitted into the tribe. A since of belonging and attention were key manipulators in one becoming a part of the group. The same process is repeated daily in settings as diverse as fraternity initiations and suicide bombers.

The corresponding part of the brain that causes addiction reacts to this cult mentality as well. Women kidnapped by enemies during tribal warfare often became loyal wives of the chief. Having once been faithful soldiers of a sworn enemy, naturalized citizens of America are fervently patriotic

It is an evolution of the brain intended for survival of the genes. Resisting capture to the point of death or denying oneself food and water in an attempt at suicide only guarantees the genetic code of the captive will be lost. Consciously or subconsciously, succumbing to your master's wishes improves one's chances of passing on one's genome. This was where Judy Miller found herself even if she hadn't realized it as yet.

The door to the salon opened and Angel Ayala entered. He pointed silently to the new arrival. It was her time. A female attendant escorted Miller to the door. Angel spoke caringly and softly to his asset. "I will see you now in my chambers. First, you must be prepared. Your gown has been laid out on your bed. Bathe and ready yourself for an evening with me." He turned on his heels and left. This was the final stage of admittance into the clan.

As Judy lounged luxuriously in her oversized tub, she began to ask questions of her attendant who continued with her charge's bathing. "I was hoping it was my turn. I know he has chosen the other girls many times. Yet I had never been the preferred one." Her fall into the total control of Angel was now complete.

"He always waits awhile to make sure you are acceptable." Meaning the brainwashing required some time. He didn't want a bucking bronco on his hands. Ayala preferred mental over physical control.

"He seems so nice but distant."

"He is a very busy and important man."

"He takes very good care of us."

"Make sure to take very good care of him." Had Miller been listening closely she would have realized the attendant had given a warning not a suggestion.

The gown that Judy slipped over her head emitted a beautiful indigo hue. The raiment was a full ruched gown with over the shoulder sleeves. The bodice fit tightly to her breasts accented with a scooped neckline. As one's eyes wandered to the midsection, the material gathered at the hips with an offset full pleat that blossomed into an ankle length hemline. Standing in front of the mirror, Judy imagined herself a complete woman.

The attendant approached and placed a ten carat diamond cut Colombian emerald around her neck. The magnificent mineral had the color and clarity as green and translucent as the eyes of a rare Jaguar. It dangled from a 22 carat braided gold chain nearly two feet in length. Chulo awaited his entertainment for the night.

When she entered the private salon of Angel she gasped for breath. A candlelight dinner lay prepared and set on a hand-carved dinner table of blackish ebony. Two servants stood nearby awaiting instructions from Angel. The master stood at his chair and motioned for the woman-child to approach. A servant held her chair.

No man had ever treated Judy Miller this nice. This was so much more than what boys could do.

"Please make yourself comfortable, Cuco." Chulo had decided on a new name for his prisoner. Everything from her past needed to be erased.

"My name is Judy. Judy Miller." A little protest could be heard in her voice.

"Not anymore. It is Cuco. When you leave here it will be Cuco, forever. You will never have that other name again. Now come let us enjoy our meal." Angel always left a little hope and doubt in the mind of the newbies.

The meal was traditional Colombian fare in spite of the formal setting. The eating of local foods acts as another instance of conditioning for the captive. The unsaid message is *this is how it is, get used to it. You're one of us now.*

"What is this?" Cuco pointed at her plate with her fork.

"Arepa con huevos. Eggs over cornbread. You will like it."

One of the servants poured strong black coffee. "Oh, I don't like coffee. It makes...."

"Drink the coffee with your arepa."

The remainder of the meal and conversation went similarly. Cuco asked what it was and Chulo described it. When the salchichas, spicy sausages, were served, Angel managed to sneak in a little sexual humor all of which went unnoticed by his forced guest.

The servant kept Cuco's glass filled with very chilled Chilean Pinot Grigio. She began to be completely seduced by the whole scene. The victim no longer thought of herself as such. She really wasn't Judy Miller anymore.

Finally desert and more coffee were served. "Eat the bunelos. You will need the energy later." Deep fried sweet muffins dusted in powder sugar sat before her.

When the meal finally finished Cuco would be no match for Ayala. Seduced, satiated, and psychologically molded to order, the girl whose parents would soon realize their daughter was missing, succumbed to Chulo's desires without even a whimper. A few drops of GHB added to her wine had only quickened the inevitable.

Chulo did with her what he had done with all of the others before her. He fit perfectly the dictionary definition of a sadomasochist. Mutual consent was not required, but in

Ayala's mind, the captives had given themselves completely to him. He did take care not to leave any physical wounds though the mental scars would be always subconsciously seeping pain until the victim's final breath. She, over time, would come to believe that what he and the other men did with her was the way of the world.

Bible school seemed a long distance away.

XXI

Wolfe wandered into Casino Bonito at Playa Linda. Kuiper was at the blackjack table. Nothing had changed. The Dutch kid might have been the worst blackjack player in Wolfe's memory. Rebelle made his greetings. Klaas Bruin stood in silent watch of his young mark.

"Hello Klaas. Hello Dirk. How are the cards running?" Wolfe knew the answer before hearing it, but making Kuiper respond, was worth the effort.

"They suck. This is ridiculous. Can't win splits or double downs. Every time I get a good hand, we push." The color of the sociopath's face looked more like that of a fair-haired Irishman eighteen hours into a St. Paddy's Day celebration.

Kuiper's constant whining had given Rebelle an idea.

"Ever play poker?"

"Sure, sure. Learned it as child. Texas Hold'em."

"Perfect." Perfect indeed, thought Wolfe. Let's get him bleeding from every orifice. "Klaas. Could you get us a private salon and dealer?"

Klaas Bruin looked none too pleased. This brash American was cutting into the action on the golden goose. The long time enforcer and pit boss knew he had little choice in the matter. "10% to the house."

"No problem. What do you say, Dirk? 25K heads up. Winner pays the house 5K. Start with dollar for dollar chip total. 500$ small blind-1000$ big blind. Blinds go up every forty-five minutes. Breaks must be mutually agreed. Compared to how your luck is running here, what the hell?"

"Sure, OK. I can't do any worse. Last hand." Of course, he could do worse. Kuiper put all of his remaining chips in the betting circle. Dirk managed to lose when he stood on 14 against a face and the dealer flipped the bottom card to expose another face.

Klaas led the two gamblers over to the private salon in the rear of the casino. Wolfe showed his 25K. The American looked at Kuiper inquisitively when the kid made no effort to show his stake. Finally, the Aruban grasped the point.

"Oh, don't worry. Klaas will pay you. Won't you Klaas?"

The bear in a 3,000$ Armani suit nodded affirmatively while giving Wolfe a less than friendly stare.

So, Wolfe thought, he's got a new cash supply. Had to come from some where. Sam will be very interested.

The dealer shuffled up and dealt. Wolfe wished this wasn't such an important game. Klaas had managed to find the most beautiful woman in the house and put her behind the table. Bruin knew the kid wouldn't be interested, but Wolfe could well be another matter. Tit for tat, as it were.

The Aruban made the same mistakes that players make when one has a little knowledge but not enough experience. One sees the same phenomena in martial arts students who learn some kicks and drops and then proceed to go out and get their ass whipped.

Kuiper's strategy was uncontrolled aggression. It were as if he hadn't gotten past the first chapter of Doyle Brunson's requisite poker tome for serious players; *Super System.* It made sense to him. His money came from selling women to a pimp and murderer. If there were any trouble, his father would cover him. He was on a free roll as far as he was concerned.

Wolfe had seen this style of play many times before. The list of poor strategy decisions included all-ins out of position with no concern for the chip count, raising the pot with any two cards pre-flop, and then hopeless follow up continuation bets even after missing the entire flop. The worst thing that happened to players like Dirk was a little bit of luck. It only reinforced bad behavior.

Only to make matters worse, the kid had a terrible physical tell. Every time he bluffed he took a sip of his drink.

Wolfe decided to play small ball. That is the strategy where one tries to keep the pots small and continually pick off ill-timed bluffs and blind steals with legitimate hands. Two hours into the game the chip count stood at 60%-40% with Rebelle in the lead.

"Why don't you go all in?"

"I just might." Wolfe peeled the edges of his cards back to expose 9-10 suited. Rebelle called the big blind.

Kuiper peeked at his pocket queens. The trouble with a reckless player is some times he actually has real cards. "All in." Dirk waved his hands over his chip pile in the universal sign among poker players meaning everything in the pot.

This was the moment for which Wolfe had been waiting. 9-10 suited connectors have the best odds of beating what seem like almost unbeatable opposing hands. It's all a matter of mathematics.

The number of outs is enhanced by being suited and by being in consecutive order. The probability of Wolfe beating an over pair going into the flop were in the mid-thirties or 2-1 in the Dutch kid's favor. Wolfe had him covered. Wolfe called. Both players exposed their hands. Rebelle could be wrong and go back to small ball if necessary. If he won, the game ended. Then the flop came.

Q-J-2 rainbow. No cards were of the same suit.

"What are you going to do now? I'm kicking your ass. Three queens." The youngster danced around behind his chair. Wolfe quickly calculated the odds.

He had 8 cards to make a straight. The probability of winning continued in the low thirties. "I've still got a chance."

Fourth street was a 3. Wolfe now had four to a flush as well. Rebelle's chances remained in the thirties. Last card coming to the felt was the river.

8 off suit. Wolfe had hit the straight. Dirk slammed his hands on the table.

"Such bullshit. How do you call with that hand? What a lucky box."

"Even a blind squirrel finds a nut from time to time. I got to go. But we can play some more at a later date. Let me know."

Kuiper waved him off and stormed from the room. Wolfe tipped the dealer but not before getting her name from her name tag. Now he had to find Klaas. It was only a short walk.

"Hey, Klaas. Got my 45K?'

"Sure, sure. Don't do that too often." His eyes averted in the direction of the front door as Kuiper bullied through players on his way to the parking lot.

"Oh, that. Got lucky. Why's it matter to you?"

"Because it matters to me. That's all you need to know. Enjoy your winnings. Is there anything else I can get you?"

"No, this will be enough. See you next time around." Wolfe walked through the door even as he felt the burning sensation of Klaas's eyes penetrate the back of his shirt. He was now on Bruin's radar. Sam wasn't going to be happy.

Wolfe crawled onto the berth next to the soundly sleeping Daga. Life from his perspective went well that day. She stirred and then rolled beneath the sheet to face him, her warm brown skin taking the chill from Wolfe's extended stay in the air-conditioned casino. Sometimes you're just on a roll.

EAGLE BEACH

Monbe dropped Sam at the taxi stand situated landside of the dancing palm tree fronds. Wolfe and Daga were easily seen.

Extended time in the tropics even made Wolfe's skin a deep brown instead of the fire brick tone he usually displayed thanks to his Cherokee grandmother. Daga, of course, showed the perfect shade of rich, dark brown one sees on the beaches of the Riviera.

Her skin color did not attract the Arubans as much as her azure eyes in contrast to her coloring and the body built by God. Wolfe usually enjoyed himself watching Daga keep the dogs at bay. It was a game with her and she enjoyed it even if the men went home more frustrated than a fisherman without fish.

Sam walked up to what were now becoming his best friends even though a dangerous line had been crossed if he ever intended to use them as intelligence assets in the future. The spy game and intelligence operations contained more twists and turns than the children's pastime of chutes and ladders.

"Howdy." Sam realized how silly the southwestern greeting sounded as soon as he uttered it. Every where he had been had left a piece inside his head.

Daga rolled over and sat up. Her suit was nothing too special today. An ivory white bikini somewhat demure relative to what she commonly wore at the beach yet it still managed to have the local pack of wolves in the tree line in a frenzy.

Wolfe answered first. "Hello, Sam. We need to talk. Hope you don't mind."

"I don't mind but I'm assuming it's rather uncomfortable for you."

"It is."

"It's your call. Daga, please excuse us for awhile. I trust you can handle the idiots over by the palms?"

"No problem. You mean the boys not the men."

"As you say." Wolfe and Sam headed to the bar.

Denys saw them coming and had the bucket of Balashis ready. He set the beer down at the bar and retreated to his seat on the cooler. Sam and Wolfe popped a couple of cold ones and swung around facing away from Denys's bartender's ears.

"What you got?"

"Good and bad. I kicked Dirk's ass last night in poker. 25K. The bad is he has more money so if your hunch is correct, there's a girl missing on the island. Second, the big bruiser Klaas at the casino is sensitive about someone else taking the kid for cash other than his operation. We're no longer strangers to him and his crew."

"Not good. Give the kid some space for awhile. We've got some other fish to fry before we get to him."

"No problem. When do we go after the little scavengers?"

"Soon. We've got to let the idea sink in that their secret scout buddy is missing as well. I believe Traficante to have been the cut-out for Dirk. As soon as Kuiper needs another victim, he'll have to do some of the dirty work himself. He'll be the one contacting the pimp. Kuiper will probably try to get the two Chowan brothers to do more. That should leave more of a trail. Right now, let's enjoy our beer and the view."

Sauria and Wolfe swung around to face the bar and ocean. Denys peeked over the edge of his newspaper. His eyes revealed feelings other than that of a happy bar man waiting on tourists. Sam read Deny's body language to be none too subtle a message that he and Wolfe could leave anytime; the bar and the island.

Early in the evening Sam made his way downtown. Sitting on a bench in the park across from the computer store where the two Chowan brothers worked, Sam ate a light snack and pretended to be absorbed in a paperback novel. Sauria repeated the stakeout over the next few days at varying times. He had the beginnings of a plan in his head.

Meanwhile, Wolfe and Daga were enjoying the island. This day the couple had switched their routine and decided to picnic at the Hooiberg, a 541 foot mount not far from the airport. Chippendale dropped the pair at the foot of the *haystack,* the English translation for Hooiberg.

"You got everything, Wolfie? Don't forget the wine." Daga looked forward to a day spent with her man that provided some respite from the reason they found themselves on this island.

"Yes, yes, I have the wine. Here take the sandwiches." Wolfe struggled with the blankets, the cooler and the chairs. He resembled the couples at the beach hauling what appeared like half of their household goods through the sand for a day in the sun. He hoped he would be rewarded for his effort with a perfect day of doing nothing. Daga had other ideas.

"Are you ready to climb the steps?" The two of them stood at the foot of the Hooiberg stairway looking up. Wolfe didn't even like the question.

"This place reminds me of Sacre Coeur in Paris. The big church on the hill in Montmarte, remember? Well, this Hooey has 562 steps."

"How do you know that?"

"I read it somewhere. Regardless, the church has around 200 steps. This is almost three times as far."

"Is my little niño already tired?"

"562 steps is exactly....." Wolfe calculated the distance into meters in his head.

"562 steps with each step being 7 inches is over 100 meters."

" 'Chu never know what 'chu will find at the end of the rainbow or the top of the mountain." Daga's blue eyes flashed bolts of passion while she exaggerated her accent for effect. Wolfe became instantly helpless.

Fifteen minutes later, the man that could not say no collapsed at the top of the Hooey. His armful of belongings fell from his grasp as well. Daga arrived momentarily afterwards no worse for the exercise. The view was magnificent.

"See, Wolfie. It is worth it, no?"

"It is worth it, yes. But we could have carried less."

Like teenage lovers, they set about spreading blankets and setting up the chairs. Daga got out the food and Wolfe popped the cork on the Chilean chardonnay.

From the top of the Hooiberg, one had a 360 degree view of the island and the Caribbean Sea. Downtown Oranjestaad easily distinguished itself from the relatively sparse remainder of the island. Cruise ships bobbed in the water as passengers streamed ashore like invading soldiers. The difference lay in the fact that these warriors rather than to kill and spread terror came to shop and spread green.

Two bottles of wine later, the lovers tumbled about wrapped in the warmth of their caring and the arms of the blanket. Exhausted, the pair napped away the early afternoon. Wolfe awoke first and carefully exited the love cocoon without waking Daga.

Relaxed and content, Rebelle lit one of his favorite cigars and settled back in a chair to enjoy the view. A Numero Tres, hand-rolled on Decatur Street in New Orleans by *los tres hermanos*, its maduro wrapper and full-bodied tobacco mixed tastefully with the figurative and literal atmosphere of the islands.

Finally the queen stirred. The sleepy blue eyes were in contrast to the very orbs that enticed Wolfe to the top of the Hooey. Even still, one of Daga's many gifts allowed her to look scrumptious 24/7. She stumbled wrapped in the blanket over to Wolfe and settled into his lap.

"Did you have a good day?"

"Yes. I had a wonderful day. You?"

"I did as well. Soon we have work, to do." The smoke trailing from his mouth turned blue as Wolfe emotionally exhaled.

"I'm looking forward to it." Daga's hatred for men who were rapists and murderers knew no legal boundaries or psychological ones.

DIRK'S HOUSE

"Neither of you have seen T?"

"Not since the other night. I spoke with one of the deckhands and he said that he saw Tony leaving with a white man, probably American, didn't seem to be under duress."

Hoeboe Chowan, the eldest sibling, always spoke for the two brothers as if they were a single entity.

"No one else?"

"Bunch of tourists. They all look the same."

"Where did they go?"

"Got in a taxi. Headed North. That's all we know."

"Well, he's missing. Not so much as a dried bone washed up at the water. No notes, no messages, nothing. Didn't pick up his last check at the boat."

"Why are you asking us?"

"Because you know him, slange!

"What?"

"Oh shit. I forgot. You don't speak civilized tongues. How does pendejo do for you?"

"I understand pendejo. We're not pigs or dummies. We have always helped you."

"No, you have always helped yourselves. If it weren't for my idea, you both would still be virgins and asking your mother for arranged marriages."

Dirk could see no headway would be made. These two were fine as diversionary tactics in a crowded bar. He didn't mind sharing his dark-haired prey with these two idiots but never the yellowtails. But as far as being functional assistants, they amounted to do nothings. They'd probably be his downfall.

Dirk needed to find Tony Traficante.

EAGLE BEACH

Daga had outdone herself. She wore only a white Brazilian thong. Wolfe, to his delight, had painted the remainder of her torso. The decoration covered only from the clavicle to the top of her bottoms but its inspiration had the intended effect. The American flag flew brilliantly that day at the beach. The forty-ninth and fiftieth stars had more prominent positions than those on the current flag. The words to the *Star Spangled Banner* might have been different had Francis Scott Key seen this banner waving in the wind.

Sam sauntered up to his friends. "Hope you're having a good day. Vacation's over."

"You got what you needed?"

"Yeh, here's the deal. The two brothers aren't twins but they might as well be. They work at the same computer store downtown. The elder brother is in charge and very protective of the younger. However, they don't work together. Some kind of extended family small business which is very usual here. One has the early shift and one has the late shift."

"Take them one at a time?"

"When?" Daga's question came nearly simultaneously to Rebelle's.

"Easy now." Sam held out his open hand. "I'm thinking snag the elder and the younger one loses it. No guidance system. He'll flip out. Let's shoot for tomorrow. Daga, you ready the boat for a cruise to Colombia and back. Fuel for motoring if necessary. Plan for a 0300h departure. About 12 hours from now."

"You and I?"

"We go downtown and wait for closing. Around 2300h. I gotta make a stop at the pharmacia.

"Imagine that." Wolfe's blood pressure rose and then settled within 30 seconds. He had that ability.

"See you in the park. Don't be late."

"Not my style."

Sam walked over to the waiting cab. Ever the perfect servant, Monbe opened the door and hurriedly drove away.

Dirk covered the beaches and hotels. No one had seen Tony. He went to the pier and asked around the Falo Fiesta. There he picked up solid information. The man talking to Dirk knew the Kuiper family and had been a deckhand at the marina for as long as Dirk could remember.

"Yeh, mon. I didn't think much of it at the time. I saw T leaving with an older white male. Like a tourist who had been drinking all evening. Not drunk but his clothing looked a little sloppy. I figured nothing. Now Tony been gone three days. It's in today's paper. Maybe a deal gone bad. You know T played around a little with the powder."

"What did this guy look like?"

"Nothing special. Wore a manila-colored guayabera. Less than six feet tall. Middle age. Light hair. Could be almost any tourist. Sure didn't look threatening."

A face flashed in Dirk's mind. No way. It couldn't be. He needed to call Denys.

"Thanks. Here's five dollars. Get yourself some beer. Don't tell anyone we had this conversation."

The deckhand mimed zipping his lips shut. Dirk hurried back to his car.

Wolfe sat down next to Sam on the bench. "He's at work?"

"Yep. He'll close up and do paperwork and then leave around 0:00h. That's when we'll make our move."

"What do you need me to do?"

"You're the distraction. Just like pickpockets. When he turns to face you he'll get a double dose of ketamine."

"Animal tranquilizer?"

"Close. I put a double dose in a solution of water and it's in a hypodermic. If I can inject directly to a major artery, say the carotid, there'll not be much resistance. Maybe thirty seconds. He'd have a better chance if he were a horse."

"Why ketamine?"

"That's what was on the shelf."

2340h and Hoeboe Chowan began turning off the lights. Sam looked at Wolfe.

"When he comes out he'll turn to his right to go to his car. You'll be standing there. He'll be startled. Ask for money. Appear drunk. Hang on him. I'll approach from his six. Get in position, now."

Wolfe ran across the street while Sam walked slowly across to eventually disappear in the shadows of the building.

Hoeboe never had a chance.

Wolfe pulled his shirttail out, turned his hat crooked, and bent over as if to be sick. The door opened and Hoeboe did not see him. The sound of the key turning in the lock was Rebelle's cue. Count to three. Go.

"Hey, mi amigo. Help a friend with some money?"

"Go sleep it off. Go back to America. Go..."

Sam struck quickly. The two men shuffled Hoeboe into the doorway and waited for the drug to take effect. After a few minutes passed, the threesome appeared on the sidewalk looking like drunk buddies coming home from a party. Chippendale pulled up to the curb.

"Oh, Mr. Sam. Your friend is not good. We go to the hospital."

"Monbe, he's had too much to drink. Take him to Wolfe's boat. He'll sleep it off."

"As you say, Mr. Sam. O Lord, don't let him get sick in my taxi! You sure he is OK? I have a cousin who's a doctor!'"

"He's not going to get sick. Just drive us to the marina."

When Monbe Chupandilla pulled up to the pier, one would have thought he suffered from an unknown ailment. Sweat ran in torrents down his smooth head; his shirt wet and wrinkled from a ten minute drive.

"I will help." Chip started to get out of the taxi.

"Stay seated. We'll take care of him. When we get out, drive off. I'm staying the night on the boat."

"But Mr. Sam...."

"Goodnight, Monbe."

Wolfe and Sam dragged the limp body up the gangway to the deck of the *Lou-Lou*. Daga met them at the gunwale.

"Let me finish him now. This is the guilty one, yes?"

"Easy, Daga. He's got some information we might be able to use. Duct tape him and we'll put him below decks. We've got twelve hours minimum before he starts to remember what happened."

Daga set about her task eagerly but it wasn't long before Sam grabbed her hand.

"Daga. If you wrap his wrists so tightly that there's no circulation while he is in this diminished state, it could kill him. Trust me. He'll wish he were dead later."

"So you say, Sam. But if there is a problem, I get to finish him. Deal?"

"Deal. Now finish up and prepare to set sail, Capitana."

Daga flashed her wide smile. The only thing she liked as well as killing scumballs was sailing.

Daga motored out of the marina and cleared the harbor markers. Wolfe and Sam scurried about the deck setting the mainsail and mizzensail. Daga stood at the wheel like a female version of the pirates of old. Hoeboe slobbered on himself lying on the galley deck.

"What's my heading, Admiral?"

"260. Punta de Gallinas. Colombia." Sam yelled back.

Wolfe glanced at Sam. "Why there?"

"I've got a little surprise for our friend. While you and Daga were playing ho-ho-ho on the Hooiberg, I was doing work."

"How'd you know we were ... Oh, never mind. Chippendale told you."

"Correcto mundo.

"What do you have in mind?"

"Ever heard of Normamyrmax esenbeck?"

"South American army ants?"

"Yeh, pretty interesting stuff. They raid other colonies and capture slaves. The colony uses collective intelligence but never sends out scouts. They bivouac for 17 day periods while in search of food sources. The queen can produce four million eggs per month while nesting. The ants devour everything in their path but only metabolize liquids. The solids are spit out in little balls of waste."

"You're telling me this because?"

"Because, I thought it apropos that Mister Hoeboe be subject to an animal that captured slaves and used them for its own purposes. A little irony, don't you think?"

"I thought we needed intelligence?"

"We can always use some but justice doesn't hurt anything as well. It isn't an instant death. He'll talk before he dies"

"You're right, Gitmo changed you."

"This is different. He's not a combatant. He's a criminal preying on innocent women. The lowest life form. His cohorts won't be interrogating our men. However, if we have our way, his buddies won't be stealing our daughters and granddaughters for profit and gratification. Think about it. Compared to what he did, he deserves it. Sometimes you have to send a message."

"Like the Colombian necktie?"

"Like the Colombian necktie."

The remainder of the voyage Wolfe and Sam sat quietly while Daga sailed with the wind at her back. The steady Easterlies provided all the force needed. The trip measured eighty miles so at eight knots headway over the bottom the *Lou-Lou* would make land around 1100-1200h. It's the time of day Sam had calculated into his plan.

Daga ran the boat aground in shallow water. Sam and Wolfe stowed the sails before attending to the brother.

Groans emitting from Hoeboe sounded more like whines. Typical, the bully is always the sissy when it comes down to it. Sam and Wolfe dragged the elder brother overboard and into the tree line while Daga secured the boat. The sun shone high in the sky.

"Over here." Sam pointed at a decaying log. The two men dropped the limp body near the rotten timber. Another high pitched moan made Hoeboe seem less human and more animal like. His behavior during his brief life did not reflect the human position at the top of the taxonomic hierarchy. He resembled much more the inhabitants of the lower levels.

A colony of ants hung from the rotten timber respiring as one body. Each individual insect clung to its neighbors with ferocious mandibles yet did the others no harm. Their collective shape took the form of the familiar inverted pyramid of the bee's nest and that of other social insects. A line of workers, uncountable in number, disappeared into the jungle mat while an identical line parallel to the first returned to the bivouac.

Sam ripped the duct tape from Hoeboe's mouth. "How you doin' punk?"

Chowan's eyes blinked open but no words were forthcoming. Instead, he gasped for air trying to get his bearings.

"I take it our friend is going to feed the ants?"

When Hoeboe heard Wolfe's question, he jerked his head around to see the colony of ants until now paying him no mind.

"No! No! You cannot do this. I haven't done anything!'

"You haven't done anything? Really? What about all those girls you drugged and raped? Some that never came home?"

"It was not rape. We got drunk and things happen."

"How about GHB? You didn't know they were being drugged?"

Wolfe joined in the fray. "When I watched your crew at work, the three of you never drank from the same shooter bottles as the women. That's rape. As bad as that is, we're really here to talk about kidnapping and eventually murder."

"Hoepoe and me never left any girls dead just drunk..."

"Quit lying. Say drugged." Sam glared at the hunter turned prey.

"Who was the last one to leave when you finished?" Wolfe suspected the answer but wanted to hear it as well.

"Always Dirk. Never us. He went first with the girls and then when we finished we would leave and he would take them back to the hotel."

"Some of them never made it back to the hotel." Sam began to boil over.

"I know. I know. But it wasn't us. When we left they were alive."

"Yeh, nice guy that you are. Alive. Just drugged and raped. Maybe you should join NOW."

"What is.."

"Shut up. I've heard enough. Here's how it's going to be. See those ants over there? They eat everything in their path including large mammals unable to escape. That would be you. We're going to sweeten the pot a little with this jar of honey." Sam pulled the jar from his pocket which had the intended effect over Hoeboe. He began to wretch.

"Kinda of like inviting the neighbors over for dinner?" Wolfe added.

"Yeh, that's it. See, the little buggers will begin to enter your every orifice. Eyes, ears, nose, mouth, anus...did I forget to mention your pisser? Up through the sinuses to your brain is a big one for them. Anyway, until they manage to sever your spinal cord you're alive unless of course they get to your heart first. Of course, you could die of shock or suffocate as the ants fill your trachea and lungs."

Being dark-skinned, Hoeboe had turned a sickly shade of green owing to his complexion. "Wha-a-at do you want!?" It was more of a wail than a question.

Sam had been waiting on this response. When the tortured succumbs completely to the torturer it is always the first question asked. Sam smiled.

"I don't want anything. I have what I wanted. I've got you. You won't be bothering naïve little girls anymore. I've got the information I needed. I've got revenge momentarily. I bet if I gave YOU," Sam shouted the word and pointed his finger, "five minutes, you couldn't come up with a real good reason not to do this to you, could you?"

"I'..ll help you get Dirk."

'That's it. That's your best pitch? He's already dead money. I'm going to get him last. When he realizes it's all over. I want to look him in the eyes."

Hoeboe began to whimper again. Wolfe pulled Sam to the side. As Wolfe spoke, Chowan tried to scramble to his feet. The effects of the drug plus his hands tied behind him and hogtied to his feet made the effort useless. Sauria kicked him in the ribs for good measure. Chowan fell back on the jungle detritus never taking his eyes from the ants.

"Dumb kid. What were you saying?"

"Are you really going to do this?" Wolfe didn't like how this felt.

"Do what? Kill him? You got a better idea? You going to baby sit him?"

"No.. I just thought…"

"Look Wolfe. You brought me into this. Maybe you thought you would catch them and the local authorities would take over. That's not real life in the third world. The whole place is corrupt. Remember, send a message. When they start realizing that they hunt us, we hunt them, maybe it'll go away. At least in Aruba. It will never, ever go away completely everywhere."

"Why don't you just shoot him?"

"I would if ants ate copper. These monsters will eat all of the evidence in a matter of days. Tape, too. I'm hoping with

Traficante gone and now the older brother, he was a rapist and co-conspirator to kidnapping and murder after all, Kuiper will get desperate. He'll need money and then we'll have him."

"What about the kid brother?"

"I'm thinking when Hoeboe fails to show, Hoepoe is done with it. That puts Dirk flying solo."

"What penalty does the kid get?"

"He's going to get a visit. He lucked out. Take care of his mother and family. Don't go to tourist bars and beaches. If anything ever happens again that resembles all of this, he's going to get another visit. I think he'll get the idea."

"Now what?"

"Let's do the deed."

Hoeboe tried to struggle, but weakened from the drugs and fear, he gave little fight to Sam and Wolfe as they tied him to the tree with jungle vines. Sam poured the honey over Chowan's head. Even as he did so, the collective senses of millions of army ants caused the insects to stop and take notice.

"Adios, amigo. Don't fuck with Americans and sure as hell don't fuck with our daughters." Sam emptied the jar and headed back down the jungle path towards the beach. Wolfe was well ahead.

The marching orders for the ant colony changed in an instant.

Sam caught up with Wolfe. "Any last words?" Rebelle asked.

"Hell no, he was pissing himself. Typical. Big bad wolf gets his ass kicked by grandma's shotgun. I did say 'adios'."

"Yeh, *to God, a dios*. It's original connotation wasn't goodbye unless one meant good riddance never to be seen again."

"I know. I thought it to be a perfect sendoff."

"So you might."

Daga stood up in the bow. "Where the hell 'chu been?" Her accent belied her grin.

"Helping stray lambs." Shot back Wolfe.

"What 'chu do with our guest?"

"As long as he stays on the continent, we'll leave him alone. I think it was a sweet offer." Sam shot a look at Wolfe and smiled.

Daga wasn't convinced. "Next time, invite me to the party. I wanted him dead."

"If he shows up anywhere again, he's all yours. Deal?" Wolfe offered.

"Deal. I hope he screws up."

Wolfe and Sam exchanged glances while wading out to the bow of the boat. A concerted push together caused the *Lou-Lou* to float free from the bank. The pair scrambled aboard and prepared to set sail.

"OK, Daga. Back to the marina. Enough work for one night. Navigate 180 degrees from your last heading."

"Sam, I like you very much but I am not a beginner at boats. Comprende? You two run the sails up and I'll head 80 degrees." Daga winked at Sam to emphasize she had already done the navigation in her head.

Wolfe watched Sam the entire way back to Aruba. He saw no signs of regret or disgust in his face or mannerisms. It were as if the OGA man had done nothing more than step on a cockroach.

Wolfe understood killing. Torture crossed into unknown territory.

XXII

Sam's phone rang at the villa. Who the hell could be calling him here midmorning, he wondered? Chippendale heard the ring and excused himself in a hurry. He didn't want to explain this one.

"Hello?"

"Sam? Is that you? It's Admiral Huck."

Shit, if he's identifying himself as Admiral Huck, this wasn't going to be good. "Yes, it is he."

"Cut the horseshit. What the fuck are you doing down there? Don't answer that! I want you to go downtown. We've got a submarine tender in port. Show them your Annapolis ring and government ID in order to come aboard and to identify yourself.. You still have those items don't you?"

"Yes, sir. I..."

"Listen up. They'll be awaiting your arrival. Report only to the XO. I need to speak with you on a secure line. I'll expect a call in forty-five minutes."

Sam couldn't believe it. The affair in Colombia was only yesterday. Even Hooters Huck wasn't *that* good. Sam jumped in Monbe's taxi and headed down the coastal road.

Chippendale was unusually quiet. He couldn't be silent forever.

"What's wrong, Mr. Sam?"

"Nothing Chippendale."

"Is your friend OK from his bad evening?"

"Yeh, Monbe. He just has some problems that are chewing him up inside."

"He needs a girlfriend. I have a cousin who would like a husband. Maybe your friend could meet her."

"He's not the marrying type. Not anymore."

"Oh, I see. A bad experience."

"Yeh, real bad. Look Chip, just drop me at the cruise port. Don't hang around. I'll call you if I need you."

"I have never given you my cell number."

"OK, fine. Go home and come back in an hour. Not before. Understood?"

"Yes, Mr. Sam."

Sauria got out and walked through the cruise terminal. After a few minutes, he walked back to the front entrance to make sure Monbe had left. Seeing no one, Sauria turned right and walked the four blocks to the gangway of the sub tender.

Guarding the deck end of the gangway were two hapless sailors assigned to SP for the port call. Sauria flashed his Department of the Navy ID.

"Permission to come aboard. I have an appointment with your XO."

"Yes, sir. Our orders are to welcome you aboard and to offer our assistance." The petty officer had been given direct orders that were to be followed without variance.

"Thank you." As Sam's feet hit the deck the XO approached.

"Welcome aboard. I will show you to my quarters where Sparky has rigged a secure line to the Admiral. May we get you coffee or something?"

"No thank you. All I need is the secure line." Sam flashed his class ring at the XO and the officer discreetly nodded.

The pair walked silently to the XO's quarters. "Here we are. I'll be waiting topside when you're finished."

Sam picked up the receiver. A young sailor's voice answered. "One moment, sir." The line went dead for a few seconds and then the sailor's voice spoke again. "Admiral Huck on the line, sir."

"Admiral Huck, sir, what can I do for you?" Sam addressed his old friend formally.

"I'll tell you what you can do for me. Tell me why I have a DJ from Aruba in detention? Are you out of your fucking mind?"

The question momentarily caught Sam unprepared but relatively relieved.

"Hello, hello are you still there? Can you copy?"

"Yes, sir. I had him picked up for a number of reasons. One, he deserved it and two, I believe he has information that could be helpful in tracing laundered money from South America to Al Qaeda."

"I thought you were on vacation? Didn't I order you to take thirty days? Are you disobeying a direct order?"

"No, sir. Not at all. I accidentally ran across this and I thought it couldn't be ignored."

"So you have one of our special op subs pick this guy up and transport him to me? Who the fuck do you know?"

"Friends at my other job."

Sam knew the veiled reference to the OGA would have a calming effect on his former classmate. It would no longer be Hooter Huck's problem.

"Well, try to get some R&R. And next time you want to pull a trick like this, I'd like a heads up."

"Absolutely, sir."

"Yeh, right. Try to stay out of trouble. Oh, by the way Sam….. happy hunting." The line went dead.

Back topside, the XO escorted Sam to the gangway. "Good luck, sir. Whatever you're doing, we need the help."

The two sailors snapped to attention as Sam approached. Although wearing his usual tropical gear, The Naval Academy ring on his finger gave Sam a virtual pass to almost anywhere in the Navy Department that wasn't classified. Even the two youngsters had noticed the XO's preferential treatment of his guest.

As Sauria's feet hit the sidewalk, he looked up to see Chippendale and his taxi waiting patiently at the cruise terminal.

At least Sauria wouldn't have to worry about Traficante for awhile. Hooter would do his best. Two were down, one hopefully neutralized, and the big fish swimming in circles, confused and hungry. The noose began to tighten in the manner that Sam had planned.

"OK, Monbe. Take me back to the villa so I can get my swim gear. Where did you take Wolfe and Daga this morning?"

"Over to Boca Prins on the SE shore. They wanted something a little different. There's large sand dunes and a little more privacy."

"When?"

"First thing this morning. Maybe eight o'clock."

Sam ran in the condo and grabbed his trunks. Back outside, he jumped in the backseat and tapped Chippendale on the shoulder as a signal to roll. Monbe eased out to the road.

"A little faster, Monbe. I need to speak to them right away."

"Yes, Mr. Sam. Whatever you need, Mr. Sam." Chip pressed down on the accelerator and the taxi lurched down the highway in the direction of the connector to the less populated SE shore.

ORANJESTAD

Hoepoe Chowan demonstrated all the outward signs of one fearing the worst. Beads of sweat ran down his forehead collecting like tributaries to a larger current until they dripped in constant rhythm from his small, brown yet beak-like nose. This torrent of perspiration sat in contrast to the cool tropical breeze of the day.

His eyes flitted side to side as if at any minute his brief life would end. Pacing the store like a circus animal anticipating its meal from the trainer, he didn't understand what had happened.

He had had the usual customers so far that day. Only one could have been a tourist. All of the others were recognizable as locals. Yet when he turned around from doing some stocking, the envelope with his name on it sat staring at him from the top of the register. He had opened it without concern but with a feeling of bewilderment about how it had found its way there without him noticing. The contents were what had brought on his current condition.

The words were not wasted. The warning had no other possible meaning. *"Dear Hoepoe Chowan. Traficante and your brother are gone because they were involved in dangerous dealings concerning Dirk Kuiper. If you do not wish to follow as well, cease all contact with the Dutch boy. Do not show this to anyone including your family and the police. Burn the letter. We are watching. This is your one and only warning. If you fail to take heed of our words, you will be next."*

Chowan saw no signature or contact number. Only the warning glared back at him. The DJ hadn't been seen for a week. Hoeboe had failed to make it home last night. His mother sat consumed by hysterics in their small home while Hoepoe worked a double shift hoping his brother would show. The delivery of the letter answered some questions but created even more.

The younger brother swung around in a panic when the sound of footsteps entered the store. It was just another local but could he be the one watching? The paranoia simmered barely below boiling.

Should he show the letter to Kuiper? Could it be Kuiper getting rid of witnesses? Had a police vigilante squad delivered it? Was it the brute and his cronies that worked at the casino? Why would they bother Dirk? He was their meal ticket.

Scared, alone without his brother, Hoepoe Chowan began to disintegrate before his own eyes. Barely in control of his hands, he lit the match and threw the burning letter into the toilet. He hoped the flushing sound wasn't his life going down the drain.

BOCA PRINS

The east side of Aruba is very different physically than the west. Subject to Easterly trade winds that blow constantly and across the great vastness of ocean thereby increasing in speed, the topography of the barren side of this Caribbean key is rugged and challenging.

Because the weather affects the terrain and the land affects the flora and fauna including humans, the personality of the place is in large contrast to the more populated and visited western shore.

Sand, caught in the grip of a wind that transports it from the Sahara Desert across six thousand miles of ocean, accumulates constantly on the facing shore. Waves pound the craggy cliffs like a million endless hammers while concurrently cutting caves in the dissolving limestone. This ravaging of the rocks is the final stage of the transformation for the numberless skeletal remains of sea creatures which eventually become part of the white-pink ribbon at the shore.

It was in these surroundings that Wolfe and Daga had come to spend the day.

Tucked behind a barricade of boulders high on a cliff, the two lovers, protected from the near gale force winds, tried to spend a day alone with forces much greater than themselves. Some things are not to be.

"There you are." Sam scrambled up the outcroppings looking like Stanley finding Livingstone in the flesh.

"Hello, Sam. What brings you all the way out here?" Wolfe flashed a crooked smile of half teeth and half chagrin.

"Needed to talk to you. Hope I didn't interrupt."

"Of course, you interrupted. It's OK. We have larger shells to crack." Daga joined the word play proving she could cut with objects other than weapons.

"Well, it's about to get hairy. Hoepoe got his warning. What he'll do with it is still in question. I got the riot act for Traficante…."

"From whom? What'd you do?"

"I recruited some help from the Agency and my boss got wind of it. I think we're OK. At least the two of you are. You're not on anyone's radar as of now."

"Thanks for the reassurance." Wolfe lay back on the blanket and stared at the sky.

"Anyway, we're coming to the big catch assuming the Chowan kid takes our advice. I wanted to tell you not to be places remote such as this and to start doing counter-surveillance in case the brother flips out and runs to Kuiper. We're on their home turf. Who knows, maybe he has the police in his pocket. Had I been here under other circumstances you two might be bobbing in the surf by now or feeding the crabs in one of these grottos."

"I wish that little boy would come after me." Daga's fighting instincts were already coming to her fore brain.

"It won't be him or Dutchie. They're both invertebrates. That's why they do what they do. They'll send someone else. Just be careful and try to be in public places with a few more bodies around. Don't trust uniforms either."

"What if we're approached? Do we defend or escape?"

"You talk. You haven't done anything. Keep your cover story. You're here to play poker and to get a tan. That's it."

"Will do, Sam. You headed back to town?"

"Yeh, Chip is waiting for me."

"Figures as much. We're coming with you." Wolfe and Daga gathered their things and like lost scouts wove their way through the brush and sand to Monbe's waiting taxi. Sam led the way.

XXIII

Sam found Daga and Wolfe sunbathing at Eagle Beach the next day.

"Don't you guys ever do anything?"

"Yes. I'm assuming you don't want the details." Wolfe countered.

Daga didn't hesitate as well. "The object is to live the good life yet be productive. The appearance of leisure is almost as satisfying as the ease itself."

"That's right Sam. Remember, work well not hard."

"OK, I give." Sauria thrust his hands out in surrender. "Something has been bothering me."

"What is it?" Daga yelled over her shoulder. The sun beamed directly on her torso and couldn't be disturbed.

"Well, we know that Kuiper kidnapped a girl recently. We know this because he has money again. Yet nothing is in the news. But Traficante's in the paper and I'm sure Chowan isn't far behind. How's that work?"

"Happens all the time, Sam." Wolfe started.

"It's why I carry my little friend." added Daga.

"Come on Sam. You know the drill. Girl has a falling out with her family. Wants to see the world. They keep here in cash for awhile or longer depending on the family's resources and the extent of the estrangement. She writes often at first. Then not so much. She shacks up either with the boyfriend who caused the alienation or the new one she found in paradise. Soon the family cuts off the money and the letters appear only when she really needs the help. They beg her to come home. She swears she will soon. Then she disappears. No one notices. No one cares. The home front figures it out six months to a year later once the case is already cold. Happens everyday all day in the third world and in some instances at locations no farther than the local bus station in the good ol' USA."

"What about the ones we hear about?"

"Bad planning on the part of the kidnappers. Instead of taking someone no one will notice they take someone who's part of a group. She fits a physical description that is desirable and the perps get careless. Soon the alarms go off. The traveling companions tell any and everyone. Television cameras appear. If the felons are extremely unlucky, the victim comes from a wealthy family with plenty of pull and resources. Those cases are a very small percentage and even those don't always get solved. The world just swallows them up."

"So these two losers we have handled will get more print then the true victims."

"Yep. Welcome to modern slavery."

Daga rolled over to her belly and glanced up at Sauria. "Sam, we'll get these guys and that's what we can do. It's a beginning."

Sam shook his head. "Glad I don't have children."

"Us, too."

"Come on. Let's go up to the bar and hang out with our favorite creepy bartender."

"You buying, Sam?" Daga flashed a smile while adjusting her cover up.

"I'm always buying for girls that look like you."

"Guess I'm out of luck then?" Wolfe gave Sauria his best stage look of forlorn.

"No, the boyfriends always get to come as well. I said I'm always buying. I didn't say I always get the girl."

"Wow, a whole generation of James Bond fans would be greatly disappointed."

"Best to keep the masses mislead."

Denys saw the threesome approaching and reached for the phone. Kuiper picked up. "The three I was telling you about. The one fits the description."

"Keep them there. I need about fifteen minutes."

Denys cradled the receiver and greeted what were now becoming regulars. "Some more Balashis? Or you want to try something a little more exotic. Maybe a little stronger?"

Daga spoke first. "I'm for it. What'd you have in mind?"

"How about a Blue Moon. Gin and Blue Curacao from our sister island. Strained and straight up in a tall glass. Slice of lime."

"Sounds refreshing. We'll take three." Why not, thought Wolfe.

While Denys went off to make the drinks Sam turned to Wolfe. "The bar man seems in a better mood today. He wasn't exactly employee of the year the last time we were here."

"Maybe he's taking some of his own medicine."

"Can't blame him. Probably gets old dealing with tourists every day but never being one."

"Yeh. It does. But it's not exactly a salt mine either."

"A lot of folks back in the states would trade places with him in a minute."

"They wouldn't last. This paradise is like all the others. Great to visit. Different to live there. Ugly, once one scrapes away the outer layer of beauty."

The drinks arrived. Daga grabbed one for herself. "Hurry hombres or you will miss e-e-ee-t!"

"She's not kidding, Sam. She's already in her drinking accent."

The three fellow sojourners tipped their glasses with one another and quaffed the bright blue liquid. A familiar voice interrupted the party.

"Hey Wolfe, fancy meeting you here." Dirk greeted them in a manner overfriendly; a manner that set both Wolfe's and Sam's radar ringing. He didn't bother to greet Daga besides a curt nod of the head.

"Hey, Dirk. Usually when I see you, you're in a casino or a bar."

"What's this? A food market? I thought I'd come see what the airplanes delivered as far as new girls. The one thing about the beach is it doesn't lie. When you meet a girl on the sand you know what her body looks like. Saves a lot of wasted effort."

Sam spoke up. "You do pretty well with that?"

"He's a lady killer. I saw him operating one night. Those girls never had a chance." Wolfe high-fived Kuiper.

Wolfe had piggybacked on Sam's lead. His dark glasses hid the real meaning of what could have been a compliment or an accusation. Wolfe slapped Dirk on the back a little too hard and smiled a little too wide. Like a friendly drunk who needs to go home, it might all be harmless. Daga ignored the conversation and ordered another drink.

Now it was Kuiper's turn. "What are you doing tonight?"

"Why? What's up?"

"I thought you might want to take a ride on the local party boat. The Falo Fiesta. You know what that name means?"

"Penis." Daga managed to get a word out between sips. Apparently falo was one word in Spanish she could hear above an alcohol distraction.

"Yeh, sorta. Phallus actually. But in Aruban slang more like *the penis party.*"

"Uh, we don't go that way. Back home that would be all guys. A dude ranch."

"No, no. no." Dirk laughed easily. "It means lots of chances to meet girls and use it."

"Oh, I see." Sam studied Kuiper. Where was he headed with this? He might as well let Wolfe keep him talking.

"Besides, all of you have already been on it, right?"

There it was. After the parry comes the thrust. If Wolfe denied it, Kuiper would know he was lying.

"Oh, that boat. Yeh, I didn't know which one you meant. Maybe there is more than one."

"There is. Makes sense." Too much sense thought Dirk.

"They've got a new DJ. The last one quit. Got off work and got in a cab with a white male middle-aged tourist. They all look alike. Actually, the description of the stranger is a little like you." Kuiper faced Sam directly. His face showed no emotion. "Hasn't been seen since."

"Yeh, I'm hiding him in my beach bag." Sam laughed.

"Not likely. Anyways, would the three of you like to go?"

"Sure why not. What time?"

"Nine o'clock. Downtown marina. See you then?" The Dutch kid turned and walked away.

He hadn't once spoken to Denys nor been offered a drink by the bar man. That had been a pretty strange encounter, thought Sam. It seemed to the old CIA handler as if they overplayed the impression of not knowing each other.

"Did we just get interrogated?"

"Yes. Don't worry. You gave as good as you got. We'll see what he has in mind for this evening. A lot of human intel is gathered in what appears to be harmless social settings. Over drinks or a meal, maybe an embassy dinner.

The funny part is that the host invites for the purpose of gathering intelligence yet usually the guest gets more benefit because the host is so hell bent trying to stimulate important dialogue without appearing to do so. I hate the damn things. Tonight will be our embassy affair Aruban style."

"Can't wait."

"Better grab Daga before she falls in her drink. I'll send Chip around to get you."

"Don't bother. We'll walk. The party boat is a few hundred meters down the quay."

"OK, see you then." Sam left for the parking lot.

Wolfe was left holding a beautiful woman unable to walk. It could have been worse.

Daga felt better by the time they reached the *Lou-Lou*. She didn't, however, make Wolfe feel better.

"Wolfie. I want Kuiper. He's the ring leader. You and Sam got the older brother. The younger brother goes with a warning that leaves the one who deserves it most; Kuiper."

"We're kind of playing by Sam's playbook. You understand?"

"I understand. But if anything changes, I want first shot on that gutless piece of sh-e-e-et!"

"I'll do my best. Come to bed. We've got things to do tomorrow."

"No. We've got things to do now."

The one thing Wolfe could never do is refuse Daga. Besides, why would he?

XXIV

Wolfe and Daga strolled along the waterfront en route to the party boat. Wolfe wore Euro-black. Daga, of course, did not.

The simple white blouse was tied in a knot snuggly beneath her breasts while the buttons, so carefully chosen and sewn by the designer, lie unused. Her brown skin, deepened in shade by time at the beach, contrasted perfectly with the color of the cloth. The shirt failed miserably or well, depending on one's perspective, in controlling the soft, easy swaying of her unconstrained breasts.

The jeans would have been one size too small on any other woman. On Daga, they seemed perfectly chosen. Her brown toes with bright red nails peeked coquettish-like from her sandals.

Sam waved to them from the quay. He had outdone himself in his choice of bad cheesy resort wear.

Instead of a loud tropical print shirt, he wore a t-shirt emblazoned with the large letters FBI. In smaller script, but still quite readable beneath the larger acronym as one approached, were the words that completed the attempted humor of the shirt; FEMALE BODY INSPECTOR. Baggy khaki cargo shorts completed the questionable ensemble accessorized by closed toe sandals worn with argyle socks stretching up his thin white calves.

Sauria smiled broadly as his partners neared. "What do think of my new outfit? Bought it the other day."

"It's certainly different." Daga quipped.

"It's all you, Sam." Wolfe bit on his lip trying not to laugh.

"Thanks. I thought after our conversation today with the idiot this would provide one more chance to get a rise out of him."

"It'll certainly create a reaction."

"Good. Come on. Let's get aboard. Let's see what he has in store for us. Oh by the way, don't stand at the hand railings once we're underway. If you want to lean, keep your back to the bulkhead. Just in case he decides to thin the competition by having one of us suffer an accident."

Once on board, Dirk greeted them immediately. The exaggerated double take reaction upon seeing Sauria's shirt changed quickly into realizing he was either the butt of a joke or Sauria simply had no idea about men's fashions. He was right about both.

"Nice shirt."

"Thought you'd like it. You know, pick up girls and all."

"Good luck." Dirk's gaze wandered in Daga's direction. His brain hit the stop button. A few seconds later, he found his words.

"You're looking better than this afternoon."

"You look the same." Daga's words carried icy contrails. Her beautiful blue eyes were dead to the world.

Her mind began to mull what she would do to him if she ever had the chance. Wolfe broke her out of the trance.

"Where are the drinks?"

"Let me get them for you."

"Sure, thanks." As Kuiper left the group to retrieve the cocktails, Wolfe gave a last reminder. "I'm sure the drinks are spiked. Probably GHB. Not enough to knock us out. Enough to make us talk. Take a sip at first and then manage to ditch the rest."

Dirk returned with the punch. "Here you go. Cheers." They all toasted. "I'm going over by that group of girls to go hunting. After all, it is the Falo Fiesta. Enjoy."

Kuiper made a direct line to the girls while the threesome tapped their toes to the beat and hung around the bulkhead.

"It's almost like he's challenging us. He wants us to see him in action. Check out our reaction."

"Pretend you don't notice. You could care less. You and Daga go dance."

"Sure. You'll be here or are we on our own?"

"I'll be here. He's already up to the third round with those girls. His drink is two or three shades lighter than the ones he gives them. Imagine that."

"We can't let him drag one of those victims off the boat."

"Go dance. I'll take care of it."

Daga dancing created a whole another venue of entertainment. Entire groups of males previously engaged in trying their best lines on half-stewed tourists suddenly became interested in the dance floor.

When Daga moved to the music it was as if she were one with the person who wrote it and the persons who recorded it. Somehow the notes entered her brain and traveled throughout her body transforming her tissues from solid to fluid. Her dancing mesmerized countless pairs of male eyes.

Wolfe managed not to embarrass himself by doing anything other than shuffling his feet. His role became that of a stage prop. It was a not too uncommon feeling to dance partners everywhere when one's partner is outstanding and one waits anxiously for the performance to end.

Finally, exhausted and dripping in pheromones, Daga made her way back to Sauria. Wolfe trailed behind in case one of the young males suffered an overdose of testosterone.

"Well, that certainly kept them entertained."

"It's not for them. It's for me."

"But they don't know that."

Wolfe and Sam surrounded Daga putting her against the bulkhead.

"You saw how we did. How'd you do?"

"Take a look."

Wolfe glanced over to where Kuiper had been. All the girls were gone except one and she proceeded to give Dirk what appeared at a distance to be a vigorous verbal attack.

"What did you do?"

"I paid one of the waitresses to follow the girls into the restroom and tell them their drinks were being spiked. Also, to warn them about similar behavior elsewhere. That one over there is the last one to give him hell."

"The waitress will tell him when she gets a chance who put her up to it."

"No she won't. I told her as long as he never finds out it's worth a hundred every time I see her. I told her I'm a wealthy American."

"In that outfit?"

"Eccentric wealthy American."

"Hope it works this time. Come on, the boat is docking. Let's get out of here before these boys can't control themselves."

As they turned to leave, Wolfe caught Dirk staring at them with a threatening look. Kuiper didn't know he had been seen.

ORANJESTAD

Next Morning

Kuiper stormed in the store. The younger Chowan didn't know what to do. His limbs stood frozen in an ice sculpture of fear and inaction. His lips and tongue, unable to find their bearings, stayed silent. Dirk's rage brought Hoepoe's speech back to life.

"What do you know?" demanded Kuiper.

"About what? I know my brother still isn't home."

"What? Your brother? What's his problem?"

"Hasn't been home in a couple of days."

"He's gone, too?"

"Don't know."

"Have you seen a group of three Americans, there's two anglo males and a woman with café con leche skin?"

"I haven't seen them in the store." Hoepoe had decided in that instant to keep the letter a secret, abide by the instructions and let Dirk take the heat.

"If you see them, call me." Dirk left the store in the same manner as he had entered; steamed.

Sam and his helpers sat enjoying late morning cocktails on the stern of the *Lou-Lou*. Dark Cruzan rum and soda with a lime made the captain's menu.

"I think you've got him where you want him, Sam. When we left last night he was pissed."

"That's what we want. Let his emotions get the better of him. Drive him over the edge."

"He's no dummy. Unless you count his lack of gambling skills."

"True, but he's in unknown waters. He thinks we're involved yet it doesn't make any sense. If he takes us on and loses, then he loses everything. The girls, the money, the toys. We might be who we say we are; some Americans coming here to gamble and catch some rays.

He'd be gambling everything on a hunch. He's sure we aren't law enforcement. Maybe he suspects us to be mob muscle of another kind. Come in and run him out of business. Like the old mafia accountants used to do."

Daga delivered another round of drinks. "I say kill him."

"Yes, Daga we know how you feel. You won't be disappointed." keeping her under control when she had her lava flowing involved high maintenance 24/7. Wolfe could handle it but it required effort.

"I've got a special treat for him. It's only a matter of time." Sam settled back onto the lush padding of the stern bench. A smile slowly creased his face.

"What's the game plan?" Wolfe leaned forward. He anticipated Kuiper's demise as much as Daga.

'The game plan, I've got. It's the timing. We're going to wait till he loses at the casino and needs more money. He'll be desperate. Afraid for his family because of Klaas and his Marseille connections. He'll need help. He'll blow through all the caution signs and red lights. Then we'll show up."

"Friends in need are friends indeed."

"Exactly."

Casino Bonito pulsated with energy in the evening. It seemed the airlines had done their part to deliver the necessary fuel to Kuiper's fire.

Beautiful woman of all ages inhabited the table games. Hopping between the green lily pads of money while dressed in assorted stages of finery or Euro-club tastelessness, they seemed unaware of all else. One could always tell new money from old. The new money dressed like they didn't have any. The old money took out loans to prove they still did.

Kuiper inhabited one of his usual spots when Wolfe moseyed up and took a seat.

"Hey, Dirk. How you doing? Sure enjoyed the boat ride the other night. You crawled in among those girls pretty fast."

"It entertained me."

"I know what you mean. Doing any good tonight?"

"Not tonight."

As if that were to ever change thought Wolfe.

"How 'bout some poker?"

"Raise the stakes? Say fifty K?"

"Sure, why not. Find Klaas and let him set it up."

Like a well-trained house pet, Bruin appeared at tableside. His pleasant demeanor no longer guaranteed. Apparently, Wolfe had gone over the Mendoza line.

"Mr. Kuiper, I'm sorry. Your line of credit is depleted."

"Well just…."

"We cannot accommodate your wishes."

Wolfe interjected. "I'll cover his ten percent if he wins. Dirk, you can pay me whenever you get it if you lose. Fair enough?"

"That's very generous of you, Wolfe. Yes, I would like that indeed."

Bruin's look at Rebelle could of boiled potatoes. Klaas had a read on Wolfe. Figuring him to be at the least a card shark and at most trouble for his golden goose, the former French Legionnaire and veteran of Algiers would keep Rebelle well within reach.

Wolfe assumed he had become persona non grata.

Klaas supplied the same dealer as previously. Wolfe's interest in her hadn't slipped past Bruin's vigilant and cold stare.

"What do you say, Dirk? Would you like to play Razz or Omaha?"

"No, thanks. Strictly Hold 'em."

"Fair enough. Say 500-1000 blinds. Go up every fifteen minutes?"

"Sure."

"Shuffle up and deal." Wolfe glanced over his dark glasses at the dealer. She rewarded him with a small smile.

Wolfe planned on playing tight-aggressive again. Only if the youngster had considered what had happened in the first game would Kuiper be likely to change his own playing style. If it went as planned, Dirk would flop around in every pot with junk cards while only winning when the cards were extremely lucky in his favor.

Wolfe let the kid have the small pots then would gut him when Kuiper chased magic cards with Wolfe holding the nuts. The entire evisceration of Dirk's stake took less than two hours.

According to Wolfe's calculations, Dutch boy would need money fast. The time to be a good friend had arrived.

"I can't believe how lucky you are!" Kuiper's rant appeared to be ending.

"Pure luck. Don't worry about it. You'll get me next time."

Wolfe paid Bruin the house 10% and generously tipped the dealer. Their hands lightly brushed as he did so. Her smile remained in place a little longer this time.

"Come on, Dirk. I've got a proposition for you. Let me buy you a drink."

"Sure, why not. Maybe I can get some of my money back."

"The drinks aren't that expensive." Wolfe slapped him on the back. The two walked toward the bar.

They settled into a corner table with the drinks and Wolfe started the pitch straight away.

"Look. My friends and I are here on business. We....."

Dirk slapped the table. "I knew it. I knew you weren't just tourists."

"That's true. However, we are in a special business. One in which we think you could be very helpful with your personal skills."

"What kind of business?"

"Well, we don't go around flapping our jaws about it. Let's say we are in the modeling business. We are in need of American models. Our backers will pay very high prices for everyone we can supply. For instance, that fifty K you just loss will be covered if you can deliver to us a beautiful woman between the ages of eighteen and twenty-two.

Now I saw you the other night on the boat and I had seen you before in the bars. You're what we need."

Kuiper thought about the offer. Chulo paid more. "How often do you need them?"

"As many as you can get. They're going to Asia. Mostly Japan and the new money in China. The wealthy executives love American woman. We give the girls 10K upfront and a one-way ticket to Tokyo or Beijing for a week of modeling. Weeks turn into months and it's not really modeling. However, from this side, it's all on the up and up.

It works like the old company store. All of their expenses are taken out of the original 10K and pretty soon they're eight thousand miles away from home and broke. No way to get back.

All you have to do is convince them they are pretty and that here's a chance to be an international model. Fifty K a head. Excuse the expression."

"I'll do it. When do we start?"

"Anytime you're ready. When you have one, you can find us around the island."

"So this is all legal? I mean, I wouldn't get in trouble?"

"Exactly. You're more like a talent scout. You convince them that they are model material and we take over from there. It is all by their choice."

"And if they show up here later, pissed off, with their parents and the police in tow?"

"You know nothing. You recruited them. They got paid. They went off to a foreign country and that's the last you heard of them. What went on over there you did not know. It didn't concern you. It's their choice."

"If this caves in, my father will come see you."

"You don't have to worry about that. We've never had a problem." Jesus, thought Wolfe. He's more careful about this than his slavery operation. Unlike his business, the girls could actually live to talk about it.

Wolfe could see visions of unlimited wealth bouncing around inside Kuiper's head. He seemed genuinely happy. Rebelle even saw the kid skip on the way to the car.

The hook had been well set.

XXV

The following morning Chip picked up Daga and Wolfe and delivered them to Sam's villa.

"How'd it go last night?" Sam handed them a couple of yellowbird drinks.

"He owes us fifty K and he's looking for models."

"Perfect. You think he bought it?"

"I super-sized it. I should have been a time share salesman."

"He's not going to hurt these girls is he? You can't let him do that!"

"Easy Daga. These girls are going to learn a lesson and not be any worse for it. We're going to play him out and then slam the trap shut. His greed is the bait."

"Sam, if he gets out of hand, let me have him first."
The queen reached back and fidgeted with her knife beneath
her hair.

"Jesus, Wolfe. How do you sleep with her."

"Uhh..... we don't do a lot of sleeping."

"I bet you don't. Anyways Daga, I got it covered. Now
you two go down to Eagle Beach and wait for him to show
up."

"We'll keep you posted."

Sam's design went as expected. Over the following days
Dirk would show up with perspective marks. Wolfe and Daga
would introduce themselves, she as a former model discovered
by Wolfe in the same manner. The girls were delighted. Kuiper
would be promised his money in a lump sum at a later date.

Sam, with Chip's transportation help, delivered the girls
to the local airport and gave each a very important lecture.

"You're not going to Beijing."

"I'm not! Where am I going?"

"Back to Ohio or Kansas or Mississippi or wherever you're from."

"What happened?"

"We saved your ass. When you got to your destination you would be eventually wholly dependent on your employers for survival. They would expect sexual favors in return."

"Oh, my God. Really?" the confused blonde brushed the hair from her eyes.

"Really. You can keep the ten K. Finish college. Start a business. Give the bank a down payment on a house. Just don't ever trust strangers again especially in a strange land. Understood?"

"Yes."

"If we see you again, you're on your own. You'll get no help from us. Now go and give your parents a big hug when you see them."

Sam shook his head. Even as the women would board the plane after each of these identical lectures, he could still see a look of minor disappointment in their faces. As if they were thinking, they almost were a model.

Now it's Dirk's time. First, another phone call to Hooters Huck.

DOWNTOWN

Dirk couldn't be silenced. "You owe me a half a million! When do I get paid?"

"As soon as we get the money. I didn't worry about it when you owed me fifty K! Our principals are arriving within the next few days. We'll take you to them and you can pick it up. It's that easy."

Daga sat silently nearby at the bar listening to the argument and wondering if she would ever get her chance with this lowest life form not worthy of the same respect as road kill.

"Look, Dirk. You're nothing but a recruiter and we are making you wealthy. Are you that impatient to be richer than your wildest dreams! Well?"

"I need the money."

"We know you do. A couple of days. Keep in touch."

Kuiper stormed away and Wolfe sat down next to Daga.

"Why do we try so hard? Just let me have him for a little while."

"Sam's way is better. If there's trouble, he's all yours."

"Good. I've got a little something for him when he's ready."

"He's ready. Stick a fork in him."

"I've got something sharper than a fork."

HUCK'S OFFICE-GITMO

The intercom squawked at Hooters Huck. Whatever it was it wasn't going to be good. "Commander Sauria on the line, sir. From Aruba." Hooters' hangover-enlarged head just swelled by a factor of three. Huck picked up the receiver.

"What the hell are you doing? Is this line secure?"

"Yes sir."

"How'd you manage that?"

"Don't ask, don't tell, sir."

"Shutup. What do you need?"

Sam outlined his plan. The admiral wasn't happy.

"If I do this for you, I'm taking your name off my Christmas card list. Is that clear?"

"Yes, sir. See through. You won't regret it."

"If I get my balls on a stick over this, I'm taking you with me. Is that understood?"

"Thank you, sir.' Sam hung up. Hooters reached into the drawer for the liquid cure.

Dirk scrambled on board the *Lou-Lou*. "Nice boat."

Daga ignored him as she prepared to push off. Wolfe did his best to keep the kid relaxed. Sam sat on the stern bench drinking rum punch in his usual attire. The sun had begun to melt at the horizon.

"So, how long till we get there?"

"About two hours. Then you'll get your money."

"I still don't understand why you can't get it for me."

"These are serious men. They want to see both of us so if we ever try to play any games there are final and lasting consequences."

"As long as I get paid. I won't be any trouble."

"Don't worry, you'll get paid. You'll feel like the wealthiest young man in Aruba." For about two seconds, thought Wolfe.

Daga made way at a heading of 270 degrees. The *Lou-Lou*, with both mizzen and mainsail full of the wind, covered the bottom at ten knots. Dirk settled down on the stern seating and waited to become rich. Wolfe waited for the action to begin.

USS HAWAII 13N 70. 2W

"Master Chief. Take us on top."

With orders practiced over hours and then years, ballast tanks blew, helmsmen pulled back on the planes, and the USS Hawaii accelerated to the surface.

With the special op tactical sub bobbing like a toy in a child's bathtub and outlined by the waning moon, SEAL Team 2 prepared to lower the ridged inflatable over the side.

Heading east for two klicks wouldn't take long. The running lights of the *Lou-Lou* were already in sight.

Operating black eliminated any well meaning accidental witnesses.

Kuiper heard the modified dual 1750 Evinrudes first. "What's that?"

"That's the sound of your money."

The inflatable pulled along side the ketch and soon a line landed on the midship.

"Who the hell are these guys?" Dirk's voice sounded pre-adolescent. He realized something didn't fit.

"They're taking you to their boat. That's where the money is. You want the money, right?"

Even money couldn't keep Kuiper from running. He turned and ran directly into the arms of Gunnery Sgt. Lopez. Smoothly and relaxed, the experienced SEAL spun Kirk around and applied the sleeper hold. The v-shape of the bent elbow positioned directly above the sternum placed the right bicep on the right carotid and the ulna of the same hand against the left carotid. The left hand increased total pressure by pushing on the ulna. The carotid arteries closed from the applied force, cutting off the oxygenated blood flow. The Dutch kid collapsed on the deck.

"Take that trash back to your boat all expense paid." Sam yelled.

"Aye, aye ,sir." SEAL Team 2 disappeared into the dark sea carrying the limp package. The trained men soon had plastic ties on both his ankles and hands before Dirk awakened to the bouncing ride back to the boat.

"Where are you taking me?" The words escaped more than they were spoken, sounding more like those of a senior citizen than of a young man.

"OK, friend. Here's the deal. You're not in charge. This isn't twenty questions. We won't kill you unless you force our hand. If you make noise or try to escape, we'll stuff your dirty underwear in your mouth and tape it shut. We don't know what you did and it doesn't matter. We're following orders. Your choice. You can vote by behaving according to our wishes or not. We will respond accordingly. Now shut up and relax."

Lopez spun around and looked out over the bow. Whatever the kid did, he fucked up big time.

As the inflatable approached the sub, Lopez slipped a hood over the package's head. Dirk Kuiper would never see daylight again.

Over the next several days, Dirk Kuiper found himself doused in institutional light, fed high calorie meals, and transported by various means while always hooded and chained. One such movement involved an eight hour flight somewhere.

POENARI CASTLE

When he de-planed the air was cold. Where could he be? The people actually gave off a different odor than he had ever smelled. By truck, he traveled up and down steep hills or maybe mountains. He felt totally helpless. This complete loss of self-determination and choice wore heavily on new arrivals as intended. The torture had already begun.

Dragged down stony steps past walls alive with the sound of dripping water, his guards threw him in a cell and slammed the door. The clanging sound of metal on metal intensified his anxiety.

His hood and chains remained in place. Over the next twenty-four hour period he eventually found sleep. The shivering and the chattering of his teeth no longer overrode his exhaustion.

Kpobb opened the cell door. What could this man have done he wondered. Definitely more than what K-Bob had been told. No matter, his instructions were specific.

"Welcome to Poenari Castle. Dracula once impaled prisoners here. We think he was rather soft-hearted. Don't you think? Oh, please don't answer. We have our own opinion.

You and I are going to become good friends. We will understand one another perfectly. I've been told you know something about money laundering? Maybe Arab charities used as fronts for terrorism?"

Mumbled sounds came from behind the hood. K-Bob motioned for a guard to remove the cowl. Dirk Kuiper, once wealthy, young, handsome, and a murderer would not have been recognized by his mother.

The brown skin of leisure in the sun had been replaced by the ghostly white of incarceration. His form, overfed and underused, now resembled a sack of melons rather than a fit young male in the prime of life. The body had been prepared for what would come next. Physically healthy individuals resisted much longer, sometimes to death.

The gag of underwear and duct tape bore proof that Kuiper had not appreciated nor followed Lopez's advice.

K-Bob ordered the guard to remove Kuiper's muzzle. "Maybe we can talk now. I am sure you are hungry and thirsty but we have business first and then maybe some nourishment. What do you think? OK?"

Animal sounds were all Dirk could muster.

"Now don't give up yet," admonished Kpobb. "You want to live, don't you?" Dangling false hope in the consciousness of the tortured, by men who knew their craft and practiced it unequaled, always accomplished the desired psychological damage.

"I guess we need to get you up and running and then we can get down to important things." K-Bob gave instructions for food, water, and blankets. He didn't want to lose this one yet.

The following days became almost the worst of Kuiper's shortened life. He knew very little. He gave them Bruin's name when asked how he spent his money. Angel Ayala's when asked the source. From K-Bob's point of view, he didn't understand why the kid had been exposed to rendition. Alas, it would not be his concern. The final stages of torture had been set.

The last mornings the Dutch kid would ever breathe, guards arrived to remove all clothing and blankets. Real torture had not been necessary in order to gain information. The scared little rabbit had talked at will.

The torture that K-Bob was about to administer, fulfilled some other need for some other person elsewhere. Kpobb played along.

Kpobb's instructions had been very specific. This particular detainee would be subjected to sodomy of every type. The Master had guards who eagerly anticipated just such sport. Afterwards, the body would become food for the wolves of the Carpatians.

In his final thoughts, it never occurred to Kuiper that he had sentenced many young women to just such treatment. Even in death, his narcissism controlled him completely.

"Why me? Why me?" he screamed as his blood flowed across the floor to lay a carpet of crimson. The cockroaches scurried to the red feast.

EAGLE BEACH

"Time to leave the island." Sam declared.

"The heat getting heavy?" Wolfe rolled over on his butt and looked up at the handler.

"Yeh. The parents and all of their money are out in force. It won't be long before our buddy Denys drops our name. I can't hold the chief off much longer. I'm sure Klaas isn't happy as well. Besides we're done here."

"Where to?" Daga seemed satisfied to know that Dirk was a done deal.

"Bogatá."

"Bogatá!? Are 'chu kidding?" Daga's accent appeared in an instant when left unguarded by her emotion.

"Sam, that's the wild, wild, west. Why are we going there?"

"You want Chulo, don't you?"

"Of course, I want Ayala."

"Then we're on our way to Bogatá. Besides, I've got an old friend there. We need her help if we are going to close this deal."

"Her help? We're not going to Bogatá so you can have a date."

"No-o-o. We're going to Bogatá because we need her help and she owes Uncle Sam. Got it?"

"Take me to your leader, Sam." The resignation in Wolfe's voice clearly displayed his acknowledgement of Sauria's superior planning and use of old networks.

"Si, take us to your leader." chimed in Daga. "I need to use mi cuchillo. It misses me. It misses blood. That is all it will miss." Daga reached behind her back and in a lightening throwing motion speared a small lizard twenty feet away on a palm tree.

"I see you still got it." Sam smiled in admiration. What a killing machine she could have been, he thought.

"Baby, I've always got it." Daga went to retrieve her knife while Wolfe only shook his head. What next seemed too obvious a question to ask one's self.

XXVI

Bogotá

Located among the parallel ranges of the Andes, the city of Santa Fe De Bogatá seemed perfectly situated to play the part of terminus to a stomach jerking amusement park ride. The flight attendant might as well welcomed everyone aboard with a cheery 'lower your safety bar, keep hands and feet inside, and secure all personal belongings.' The GIV-X Gulfstream chartered jet and pilot struggled against the changing air patterns and associated topography eventually coming in over the Cordillera Oriental from the East.

This city, racked by drug cartel terrorism, kidnapping, and just plain murder, could otherwise be the jewel of South

America. Large expanses of skyscrapers point eagerly upward each one reaching higher than the next.

Surrounding the glass palaces are small neighborhoods reminiscent of nineteenth century Hollywood re-creations. One might expect to see Marlon Brando or Anthony Quinn peeking from a darkened doorway while brandishing pistolas and layered with bandoleros.

In peaceful contrast, perfectly cobbled alleys are lined with an endless parade of balconies covered in bougainvillea.

The DEA had stashed Griselda in one of the small apartments on Calle Colón. Her residence made more ironic by living in one of the most dangerous cities in the world. Putting Senora Blanco here was akin to starting a fire to extinguish one. Some of her dangerous neighbors knew full well the war that would begin if someone foolishly tried to put a hit on the quiet widow in the small apartment at Number 17 Calle Colón.

Sam knocked on the door; twice, short pause, twice again, and then a continual repeated single rap without pauses.

The door, decorated by an oversized hand-carved crucifix, swung open. The years of murderous business and cocaine had not been gentle to Griselda.

Never a beauty, Senora Blanco had, by her lifestyle, exaggerated all of her poor features that even youth had not been able to hide. Long tangled strands of gray hair fell over her face hiding none of her worst attributes but only adding to her repulsive looks.

The large head sat atop an equally grotesque body. These two features were in proportion unlike her others. An enormous brightly printed shift hung from her shoulders in a shapeless attempt to cover the large pendulous breasts These dual witnesses to mass and gravity were the coup de grace of her genetic disfigurement.

Her personality had not faired any better. "Hola, Sam. I recognized that knock after all these years. Who are your compadres?"

Griselda wagged her head in the direction of Wolfe and Daga who appeared like small children peering around their parent's waist. Sam had suggested standing behind him as Senora Blanco might come out armed.

"They can be trusted. May we come in? I don't like standing out here in front of your door. Some of your friends or enemies might take offense. By the way, where's your bodyguard?"

"They come and go. They check up on me. They have the sat phone. Do I have a choice about our visit?"

"No."

"Then bienvenidos. Su casa es mi casa."

The threesome ushered themselves into the studio apartment and took seats where they could find them. Griselda sat a bottle of Reposado tequila and limes on the table and lit a Cohiba cigar. Sam smiled. Whether you liked her or not, no one ever argued the point that Senora Blanco was a real American character.

"I knew our little telephone conversation would not be the end of it."

"See, you said I never come to see you. Now I am here."

"Well yes, I had other things in mind." Rich, blue smoke curled from her lips into the space between Sam and Griselda.

"I do as well."

"Speak. I find myself forever in the service of you and your government."

"Oh, come on my Griselda. Compared to the others of your kind, you live quite well."

"So I do. A velvet cage yet still a cage."

"A major difference considering your past. Enough of this, Griselda. I came here for help only you can give me."

"Sí, the Sam of old. The supplicant. I like it. What is it that you need?"

"I want you to contact some old friends."

"I have many."

"Some would disagree. Do you remember *Search Block*?"

"Yes, I was here by then. The operational code name for the hunting of Pablo Escobar. The Cali kingpin. Sí."

"Well those guys, the government soldiers, were trained by Delta Force. Do you remember how it turned out?"

"They trapped and killed him in broad daylight."

"Yes, but before that, the group as a whole had been unsuccessful. Do you remember what changed it?"

"No, but I'm sure you will tell me."

"Los Pepes. The vigilantes. The authorities suspected them of being members of Search Block. They killed corrupt judges, members of Escobar's extended family, his accountant. The list goes on. Then all of a sudden, Search Block got actionable real time intelligence about Pablo's movements. A short time afterwards, Escobar's bullet bloated body is seen on worldwide TV."

"And this has what to do with us? Here in this room?"

"I need you to contact them."

"For what reason? No, let me guess. Perhaps a ten year reunion?"

"At least your humor entertains. No, it's one last operation. It is Ayala. Up in the mountains. He's gone too far. He's enslaving and then killing young American girls. It was only going to be when, not if, someone responded. In this case, it is us." Sam swept his hand in an arc. Wolfe and Daga nodded.

"Oh, you definitely need these men. Chulo is well guarded. So my sources say."

"Griselda, we know you send him women as well. Poor street urchins and drug addicts. We look the other way. But no longer."

"Ah, yes. American lives have more value than others. I had forgotten since my time in Miami. We could kill Colombians and Mexicans no problem. But kill a cop or college kid, aye, aye, aye, how you say, the roof caves in."

"Yes, the roof caves in. And so we find ourselves here. Will you do it?"

"If I choose not to do so?"

"It will be your last decision without bars between you and the outside world. You'd go straight to the Supermax in Colorado."

"Sam, you always had a way with words. So subtle."

"Your answer?"

"Of course, I will help. Come here tomorrow. Same time."

"No double cross."

"No double cross, mi amigo. I like my life here."

Sam, with Wolfe and Daga trailing him, bid his old nemesis and informant goodbye.

No one ran a double cross as well as Griselda in the old days of Miami. She had eliminated half of her competition by informing to Sam. In return for her services, Sam had allowed her crew to exist until the last. Then her gang fell into law enforcement hands. Many of them received life without parole and a few the death sentence.

Griselda benefited from her association with Sam. She got life without parole in absentia. Law enforcement searched endlessly for her. Sam had her transported out of the country. The underbelly world of espionage and drug cartels never operated with the concept of loyalty. Everything had a price.

The threesome checked into the Hotel Pirata around the block from Griselda's safe house. Wolfe liked the name. Sam liked the location. Daga liked the bar.

The older gentleman behind the counter brought over a full bottle of Cacique aged rum. The cane juice liquor arrived with a pitcher of ice, a six pack of coca-cola, a plate of limes, and the necessary glasses. The group chose the singular table in the corner.

"One stop shopping." Wolfe looked at Daga.

"What? I decided to save the old guy some steps." The mock indignation in her voice only made Daga sexier to Wolfe and any other men within ear shot.

"You're so thoughtful when you're thirsty." Sam chided.

The name of this particular watering hole, *Botella de Rum* in the Pirate Hotel, did much to explain the faux Blackbeard décor and the Jolly Roger bev naps.

"You think we're OK for tomorrow?"

"Yeh, Wolfe. We've got Griselda by the shorties. Nothing she can do but play along."

"And if she chooses to not play along?"

"She'll play along. She survived Miami in the eighties. Very few others are alive to dispute her ability to watch out for Griselda. She's got too much to lose."

"She's old. Maybe she doesn't care?"

"She cares. She'll die of old age if she has the last word. We're OK."

With the bottle of rum finished, the group headed up the staircase. Hands, resting on the wood carved in the manner of a captured corvette's gunwales, gave necessary support. The drunken conspirators disappeared into their rooms.

Wolfe awoke with a start. The popping sounds of small caliber rounds followed by the high pitched whining of the ricochets off of the cobbled street and building facades were continual. Maybe a ten shot burst and return fire every fifteen minutes or so became the average. Cowering by the windowsill, Wolfe checked the street. No lights appeared in the windows, the people behind the curtains not wanting to be targets or witnesses. Thugs defending territory with undisciplined fire became Wolfe's evening serenade. Daga never budged.

Sam met them in the hotel lobby in the morning. The previous night's sounds were now gone and replaced with the rattle of street vendors and pedestrians.

"How'd you sleep?"

"How'd I sleep?! You're awful cheerful this morning, Sam. You didn't hear all the gunfire?"

"That's Colombia. It might as well have been castanets. Puts me to sleep."

"I didn't hear anything." Daga smirked.

"Of course not, you were dead to the world. Never mind. Are we ready for your friend?"

"When we get there." Sam walked down the thin sidewalk leading the pack. Wolfe and Daga followed five paces back. Either from training or imitation, people walking in clusters usually didn't have a happy ending in this part of Bogotá.

Sam repeated his knock and this time a man dressed in night op utilities opened the door. The business end of his M4 assault rifle, safety off, pointed at Sam's midsection.

"We're here to see Griselda." Sam flashed the innocuous ID of an USAID representative. Carrying legitimate CIA credentials did not increase one's life expectancy in the third world. USAID had long time ago become the cover ID.

The guard let them pass and closed the door behind his self as he took up post outside.

"Good morning, Griselda." Sam greeted Senora Blanco. She smiled without showing her teeth.

"Allow me to get right to business." The beads separating the living room from the sleeping quarters rattled. A man entered the space. Griselda did the introductions.

"This is Colonel Cabazón. You might know him better as El Jefe de Los Pepes."

Tall and with the bearing of a man who had spent his entire life in the military, the colonel nodded his head. Then he spoke.

"Please, permit me. I will speak in English. If I have trouble, our friend Griselda will help."

"Certainly." Sam didn't worry about twisted translations. Daga made excellent backup.

"You need our help?" The salt and pepper moustache twitched at the corner of his mouth in perfect meter with each syllable.

"Yes. We are willing to pay. One million US$. No questions asked." Wolfe and Daga tried to control their facial expressions, totally surprised by Sam's offer.

"Where will this occur?"

"In Colombia. Punta Gallinas and nearby. It is dangerous but it pays well."

"Who?"

"Does it matter?"

"We have families."

"There'll be no witnesses."

"Payment?"

"One half before, one half when finished. Cash, of course."

"How many men do we expect to encounter?"

"Maybe twenty. Well-armed but poorly trained. Surprise will be on your side."

"When?"

"As soon as you're ready. I can provide real time full motion video up till and during the operation for your tactical purposes."

"How do you propose to do such a thing?"

"That's not your problem. What is your decision?"

"Trato hecho. It's a deal."

"One more thing. We go with you."

"That might cost more."

"It won't cost more. You've heard the offer." Sam turned to leave. Wolfe and Daga stood.

"Sure. OK. It's your lives. My money?"

"Call Griselda. She will know."

The Colonel's eyes flashed at Señora Blanco's face. She nodded in affirmation.

The next few weeks Sam disappeared for most of each day. Wolfe and Daga lounged at the pool and depleted the local rum supply. Each evening, Sam would return and brief the pair on their roles in the impending assault. Ayala did what he did in oblivion.

CASA CONCHA

Chulo enjoyed another day. Three Arab princes from the family of Saud had paid a visit. The money was good but the Arabs always destroyed the women. Three of Ayala's best were now relegated to the cells below. Three yellowtails were now categorized as worthless for everyone except the campesinos. Not to worry, he thought, five million dollars would buy fifty more from the degenerate Dutch kid.

Judy Miller had not been one of the unlucky ones. Ayala still found some interest in her. However, she soon would be on the market for his high rollers and, he, Chulo, would wait for another to replace her.

The drugs which were administered daily to Judy performed their handiwork as expected. The oxycodone given by her matron each morning in the form of *vitamins* kept her easily controlled. Her addiction along with the psychological manipulation made her a perfect product for Ayala's operation.

She liked living here. The only thing kind of strange was the sex, but Angel had told her that these are tastes that all men have and it's the woman's place to follow and submit. What she didn't know was that the good days were numbered and the end of her days not far removed.

A CIA operated Predator circled almost silently over the fortress. The infra-red cameras whined as they transmitted live video. Hooters Huck and Sam were both all-in.

Ten klicks away outside the small town of Ríohacha, Colonel Cabazón prepared his men. Sam watched in wonderment. The same training techniques used by Delta Force were now being seamlessly imitated by these men. The soldiers, well-trained before, used these weeks as a refresher course.

The Colonel had built a mock-up of Ayala's fortress so the men could practice timing, position, distances and tactics. The unknown interior of the target loomed large as an obstacle. Such is the art of war.

Sam watched as the sniper teams practiced at targets up to five hundred meters in distance. The mangoes substituted for human heads dissolved in silence. Chulo's guards didn't have a chance.

"Where'd these guys learn to shoot like that?"

"Do you know who Lyudmila Pavlichenko was?

"Female Russian sniper, WWII. She had 309 confirmed kills. Mostly around Odessa."

"Very good, my American friend. She received the Gold Star of the Hero of the Soviet Union. They put her face on a postage stamp as well."

"What does that have to do with these men?" Sam waved his hand at the sharpshooters.

"After the war, she went on a goodwill tour to the USA and Canada. She made frequent stops in Cuba after Fidel took power in 1959. Had the USA invaded Cuba after the Bay of Pigs, your men would have been up against the best trained sniper corps in the world."

"So she trained the Cubans and then the Cubans passed on the training to your military?"

"Correct. We use Delta force tactics along with Russian sniping and counter-sniping techniques. Remember, East and West have been fighting over South America for a long time,. We sat back and took advantage of the offers."

"So Search Block was about killing not capturing?"

"Of course."

The final training time passed quickly and the assault on Concha Casa and its chambers of horrors would begin soon.

Sam briefed Wolfe and Daga. "The two of you will be at the gate to the compound waiting for me. If I don't return within thirty minutes, leave without me. Your tasked to exit with any female packages I can salvage. I'll be performing a type of triage. I'll only bring the ones who have a chance of returning to a normal life and I have to make that call in split seconds. It's the best we can do. We're really not there to rescue people. We're going in to finish Chulo. If we find some possible survivors, so be it.

The two of you will escort any females back to our departure point and bring them to the Colonel's camp. Questions?"

"Good luck to us." Wolfe mumbled.

"Wake up 2300h. Push off 0200h. Operation Cracked Shell begins in earnest 0330h. Get some rest."

CASA CONCHA

The first head of a sentry exploded in a pink misty cloud at 0330h. Using a VSS Vintorez Russian model nine millimeter, the former Los Pepes member smiled to himself at kill number one. The silencer and flash suppressor mounted on the muzzle gave no hint of his whereabouts. Two more sentries fell as Colonel Cabazón's assault team casually walked up to the gate and opened it with a set of bolt cutters.

The bodyguards lounging on the veranda went down in puffs of smoke and blood as silenced nine millimeter Grach handguns snuggled to their ears. The shootout inside began more like a fiesta.

The chink-chink sound of AK-47's became like sounds of nature, easily heard but soon passing into one's subconscious. Rounds whizzed through the air like agitated bees. These stings would not be just bothersome but deadly.

Chulo awoke to the gunfire. He reached for his silk robe and started to open the door and then hesitated. Who could it be? Rival criminals? The authorities? No way. He had paid off everyone from here to Bogatá. Angel Ayala crawled under his four-posted bed and shook in fear.

Bloody bodies torn in pieces by the technology of war dropped in pairs and groups. Los Pepes eliminated all resistance in three minutes. The room to room search began.

Sam stumbled upon the basement. The scene brought bile to his lips. He fought it back down his throat only to vomit as he walked when the next victim came into view. In his heart he felt sadness for them and their families but in his brain, intellectually, he thought of dogs needing to be put out of their misery.

The souls of these women had been stolen by Angel Ayala. Their time and space in this life were no longer worthy of the pain necessary for survival. Sauria bounded up the stairway to the living quarters. The captives below remained as they were.

The Colonel greeted Sam at the top of the stairs. "We found three females in relatively good condition. They didn't want to come with us."

"That's understandable. They've been Stockholmed. Brainwashed. Did you find Ayala?"

"Si, he's over there in the corner shaking."

"Of course, the coward is. Have some of your men take the women down to the guard gate and give them to my compadres. There's a situation in the basement that I believe is best handled by you and your men. You will understand when you see it. If you do as I think you will, torch the place when you are finished. I have complete faith in your judgment."

The Colonel gave orders and his assault team scrambled down the stairs. Sam walked over to Chulo.

"Stand up." Chulo cowered beneath his robe hiding his face. No movement was forthcoming.

"Stand up! Levantarse¡ Stand up!" Sam commanded again. Sauria reached down and pulled the robe away from the face.

Chulo stood on quaking knees. He began to speak. Sam held up his open hand.

"You have been found guilty by a tribunal. You have committed crimes against humanity. The penalty is death. You deserve worse." Sam stepped back and pointed the German police pistol at the head of the pimp. Ayala fainted in the corner. Sam walked over and pulled the trigger twice. The rounds entered just behind the left ear. Sam spit on the corpse. He wondered if the animals would even eat the body.

The suppressed sounds of silenced handguns echoed up from the cages. Sam could visualize Cabazón's men going from cell to cell killing the captives and freeing them from their torture. The deed done, Sam walked slowly to the gate. His head hung low. The disgust for what is necessary sometimes could not be hidden.

Wolfe and Daga greeted him and the group walked back together to the five ton troop carrier. Three women huddled in the back under the scrutiny of one of the Colonel's men.

Judith Miller wondered what she had done wrong.

Where were they going?

Where did Angel go? Who are these Americans?

XXVII

Ohio State Institute of Mental Health

Office, Dr. Steinberg

"How is she doing?" Mr. and Mrs. Miller huddled together on the standard issue faux leather and chrome chairs. It had been six weeks since they had gotten their daughter back but she still wasn't the girl they had raised. They hoped today would be different.

"She is still struggling. She wonders why we are holding her here. As I have explained in the past, we basically have to re-program her for society using techniques not so very different then those used by her captors to make her as she is. We must be patient." Dr. Steinberg sat behind his desk knowing his answers were not what the couple came to hear.

"Will she ever be normal?" Maude Miller asked.

"Well normal has a large range of definitions..."

"Dr. Steinberg," interrupted Jack Miller. "We know she has been through a lot. What we mean is, will she ever get married? Have children? You know, be a regular person."

"That is our hope. As we have discussed, she is physically OK. The mind is a tricky thing. With time and effort, I think she can come home to live with you again. Whether or not she ever has a healthy sex life is completely up in the air.

Think of it like a house pet that has been abused. Just the sound of the newspaper causes it to scamper and hide. In her case, demons from the past may interfere with her relationships. We honestly don't know."

"What good are you to us?!" Maude Miller screamed and then hid her face in her husband's weathered neck. He glanced at the doctor.

"We're sorry, Dr. Steinberg. We're just working people. We tried to give our daughter things we never had. Nice clothes. Travel. Then it backfired. We got to trust you. There's no place else to go."

"I understand."

"Can we see her?" Maude's head popped up to ask.

"Not yet. It's too soon. Continue to write. Tell her you love her. Send her childhood photos. Maybe next week." Or maybe never, the doctor thought.

Maude and Jack Miller excused themselves and slumped out of the chairs to the door. It were as if all life had been sucked from there beings. As parents, they were only slightly better off than those families with no bodies to bury only a lifetime of wondering.

At least, the Millers knew.

TIKI HUT, HILTON HEAD ISLAND

"Sam, we can't thank you enough." Wolfe sipped from his drink.

"I'm glad I got involved. I felt like I was doing some good."

"I only wish I could have done more. Especially with Chulo." Daga's eyes narrowed. "That pimp will never know how lucky he was."

"Trust me. He got his. The problem is the cultural setting that allows that sort of thing to happen. In the first decade of the twenty-first century, people are still being enslaved, used up, and then disposed like trash. Usually women and children. Usually for cheap labor and prostitution. Sometimes as boy soldiers."

"What about Judith Miller?" Wolfe had last seen her getting on a plane escorted by US embassy personnel.

"She's back home. Hospitalized. More for psychological problems than anything else. She was one of the lucky ones."

"If you call that lucky."

"Well, she back home with her parents and they love her. Hopefully, it'll all turn out OK." Sam slugged down the rest of his Cuba Libre to help hide his own disbelief that she would ever fully recover.

"Where you headed to now, Sam?"

"Back to Gitmo. I've got a few more years before I can retire. I'm asking for a transfer as soon as I arrive. But I don't know. There doesn't seem to be any end to this war on terror. There is a third of the world's population being taught from early age to hate the West. Being taught by their religious leaders, of all things.

Millions of young men coming of age in a part of the world that has never been anything but an economic disaster except for the privileged royalty and their oil. They have no jobs. They can't afford wives. War is all around them. Human life carries little value. It's so easy to influence them.

What about you two?"

"We're thinking of the desert. Our desert. Nevada somewhere."

"Si, Sam. My Wolfie has grown tired of the humidity and the hurricanes."

"Good luck. I got to go. I got to catch a plane." Sam stood and made his farewells.

"We'll still know where to find you two. The desert's not that big. And when you get tired of that, I know I can always find you here at the Tiki Hut."

"Probably so Sam, probably so." Wolfe and Daga gave him one last hug and watched as Sam, wearing his Jimmy Buffet ensemble, rumbled off the deck.

Wolfe ordered another round which Daga gladly accepted. The sounds of local musician Rob Ingman danced through the air. The song he was playing, *Over-medicated*, off his last hit CD titled *Bacardi-ac Arrest*, seemed perfectly appropriate. Wolfe and Daga had a lot of forgetting to do.

Sun toasted and rum roasted, Wolfe and Daga walked back to their room at the Holiday Inn. Wolfe was out to the world in minutes. Daga tossed and turned beneath the cool sheets. Finally, sleep overtook her.

Early in the morning, well before sunrise, Daga awoke with a start. The sliding glass door was open and wet air blew in from the water. She reached for her knife. Then she heard the familiar giggle.

"Hee-hee-hee. You won't be needing that, dahlin'."

"Lou-lou. I've been dreaming of you."

"I know you have. It wasn't a dream. You have powers even you don't know. That's is why I am here, baby." Lou-lou sat in the corner chair dressed in white linen through which her soft brown skin shone. The last light of the full moon through the window gave her face an eerie presence.

"I haven't seen you since New Orleans."

"You haven't needed me. You think you need me now."

"I can't get that girl Judith Miller off my mind."

"You are a voodoo priestess. You are stunningly beautiful with blue eyes. Your village knew you were special immediately at your birth. Do what you have always done. Exercise your powers, your special gifts. That young girl needs you, dahlin'.

Here. I brought you some supplies. All you need for white magic. Some bones, a lock of her hair, ivory dice, a bottle of rum, and candles." Lou-lou handed over a white lace drawstring handbag.

Daga looked in the bag and glanced up at Lou-lou. She was gone. The curtains still danced in the open door.

Daga performed the spell. The one she hoped would help Judith Miller. Time passed quickly and Daga collapsed back on the bed in a puddle of sweat when she had finished. Wolfe never stirred.

The next morning Daga's eyes opened. Where was she? She remembered the previous night. She jumped out of bed.

"What's a matter, honey. You're not getting out of bed before we have a chance to enjoy ourselves, are you?" Wolfe rolled over to see what caused the commotion.

"It ees nothing. I just..." All of the voodoo materials were gone. Had she dreamt it?

Daga glanced at the door. It stood open welcoming the breeze. Maybe Wolfe had opened it.

Wolfe wondered why the heavy accent so early in the morning. "What's bothering you? You sound upset."

"Did you open the door?" Even as she asked the question, Daga glanced down at the carpet leading to the balcony. Petite, sandy, barefoot outlines led first in and then out to the deck. A smile crossed her face.

"Come on, baby. Me and you. Now. It's the only way to start the day." Wolfe teased.

Daga turned and took a flying leap on to the bed. Wolfe wasn't sure what happened, but whatever it was, the she-cat was out of the bag.

Eight hundred miles away and a few days later, Judith Miller greeted her parents. Her recovery had been nothing less than dramatic. The doctors all concurred. As the happy family embraced and left the hospital, Jack Miller noticed another patient.

She sat on a bench in the sun wearing a white linen dress and laughing to herself.

"Did you see that little girl? The one on the bench."

His wife and daughter didn't hear the question. They were too occupied with their own happiness.

"The light-skinned African girl. I hope they can help her. She was just laughing for no reason." Still he seemed only to be talking and not being heard.

Jack Miller looked back at the bench. The strange girl was gone. But he could still hear her laughter from around the corner of the building.

"Hee-hee-hee."

Jack Miller didn't care. His wife was happy and his daughter back where she belonged. He turned and caught up with his family.

1554589

Made in the USA